Dear Reader,

It's such a thrill to be releasing *Sheikh Boss, Hot Desert Nights* for Harlequin's sixtieth birthday celebrations. The story features a hero the girls in the office assure me is my hottest sheikh yet!

Who wouldn't be inspired to be involved in such a wonderful publishing tradition? Harlequin's anniversary of sixty years of reading pleasure is an outstanding landmark, and one I'm very proud to be part of.

No wonder I love romance—I met my husband on the tiny Mediterranean island of Malta on Monday and was engaged to him by Friday. We were married within three months, and three wonderful children later we are still very much in love.

Being part of Harlequin's history is both a privilege and a pleasure, and my greatest enjoyment comes from sharing that pleasure with you, my readers.

I'm often asked, "Where do you find your inspiration?" The answer is, from you. I want you to have the romance of your dreams, and I strive with everything I've got to make sure you get it.

I love nothing better than hearing from my readers around the world, so please do drop by my Web site, www.susanstephens.net, where you'll find contests and news.

With my warmest wishes to you all,

Your friend and author,

Susan Stephens

Even if at times work is rather boring,
there is one person making the office a whole
lot more interesting: the boss!

Dark and dangerous, alpha and powerful,
rich and ruthless... He's in control, he knows
what he wants and he's going to get it!
He's tall, handsome and breathtakingly attractive.
And there's one outcome that's never in doubt—
the heroines of these sparkly, supersexy
stories will be:

From sensible suits...into satin sheets!

A brand-new miniseries available only from
Harlequin Presents®!

Susan Stephens

SHEIKH BOSS,
HOT DESERT NIGHTS

Undressed
BY THE BOSS

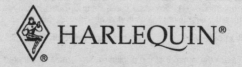

HARLEQUIN®

TORONTO • NEW YORK • LONDON
AMSTERDAM • PARIS • SYDNEY • HAMBURG
STOCKHOLM • ATHENS • TOKYO • MILAN • MADRID
PRAGUE • WARSAW • BUDAPEST • AUCKLAND

Recycling programs
for this product may
not exist in your area.

ISBN-13: 978-0-373-12842-6

SHEIKH BOSS, HOT DESERT NIGHTS

First North American Publication 2009.

Copyright © 2009 by Susan Stephens.

www.eHarlequin.com

Printed in U.S.A.

All about the author...
Susan Stephens

SUSAN STEPHENS was a professional singer before meeting her husband on the tiny Mediterranean island of Malta. In true Harlequin Presents® style they met on Monday, became engaged on Friday and were married three months later. Almost thirty years and three children later they are still in love. (Susan does not advise her children to return home one day with a similar story, as she may not take the news with the same fortitude as her own mother!)

Susan had written several nonfiction books when fate took a hand. At a charity costume ball there was an after-dinner auction. One of the lots, "Spend a Day with an Author," had been donated by Harlelquin author Penny Jordan. Susan's husband bought this lot and Penny was to become not just a great friend, but a wonderful mentor who encouraged Susan to write romance.

Susan loves her family, her pets, her friends and her writing. She enjoys entertaining, travel and going to the theater. She reads, cooks and plays the piano to relax, and can occasionally be found throwing herself off mountains on a pair of skis or galloping through the countryside.

Visit Susan's Web site, www.susanstephens.net.
She loves to hear from her readers
all around the world!

For all those who like their bad boys
safely corralled between the pages of a book,
and for Bev, whose face lights up
when I mention the word "sheikh."

CHAPTER ONE

SHE had a backpack the size of the world. Hoisting it off the luggage carousel, she almost knocked out the eye of the woman standing next to her. Buckles and straps jangled from it, along with a rope, a waterproof bedsheet, and a pair of sand boots. She had her hair scraped back and a camouflage hat with a highly becoming neck-flap crammed on her head.

Hearing she was to travel to the interior of A'Qaban as part of her job as marketing executive to that country's development agency, Casey had ditched the power suit and Jimmy Choos in favour of a safari suit and sandproof knickers. But this wasn't an airstrip in the furthest reaches of A'Qaban, but A'Qaban International Airport, where the desert came in bijou-sized pieces, each grain of sand polished to a heady sheen by the world's top designers.

As with any other project she undertook for the company, Casey had researched this one thoroughly. It had only been on the point of boarding the aircraft that she had been told her itinerary had been changed—and by none other than the recently crowned King, Sheikh Rafik al Bad-Boy himself. Apparently His Majesty had insisted on meeting all his key employees before ruling the country took his eye off the business.

Surprised to find an underling like herself under the spotlight, Casey had allowed herself a momentary glow, until it was pointed out to her that Raffa, as the Eton educated and Special

Forces hardened Sheik preferred to be known, was well into weeding out the weak links in his organisation. So, here she was, dressed like a park ranger in the midst of Glitz Central, and with no office clothes to save the day.

She had a wardrobe full of smart business suits back home, but what was the point in kicking herself? She was here and she had to get on with it, Casey reflected, hoisting her back-pack into a more comfortable position. The Sheikh of A'Qaban was known to test his employees to the limit and she should have had it covered. She might be at a disadvantage, but not for long. As soon as she cleared Customs it would be all about the shopping mall.

Could sexual heat pass through glass? Watching Casey Michaels cross the baggage hall, he thought it could. Even in that outfit she looked good...funny, but good.

How could she not look better than the uptight fashion victim he'd taken a look at in her file? He could see that was an old photo, way out of date now. She had blossomed since it had been taken—more flesh on her bones, and way more blonde hair falling down beneath her ugly hat. That, combined with the good-humoured curve of her lips, the direct, unflustered gaze and the determined stride, made for quite a package—even if that package was bundled up in the most un-flattering of clothes.

Her clothes could change. He was wearing jeans and a top for this reconnaissance mission. Official robes were a costume he wore when appropriate—just as Casey would step into a different role when she put on a severely tailored business suit.

The thought of unlacing those office stays and discovering the real woman underneath was an image that pleased him perhaps more than it should have done. Thumbing his sharp black stubble, he weighed up the supple frame beneath the un-flattering safari suit. Virginal innocence sang out loud and clear.

And he never mixed business with pleasure.

He turned his mind to the point of Casey's visit. Could she inspire? Could she lead? Was she prepared to fight for her people? Those were the things that mattered to him. With the livelihoods of thousands of employees at stake, only the strongest executives would survive his cut.

But she intrigued him. He pulled back from his vantage point. It was time to move on if he wanted to keep an eye on Casey's progress. Thanking each of his customs officials in turn by name for their hospitality, he left the viewing room. He felt super-wired—the way he always felt when the hunt was on. And there was nothing wrong with that. He needed a little craziness in his life, a little freshness.

In his *life?*

Business *and* pleasure?

A glint of humour was in his eyes as he joined the bustle in the arrivals hall. Some people recognised him; some stood gaping; some didn't know him from Adam. The question was, would *she* recognise him?

His ever-present bodyguards knew to remain invisible. Taken out of context, he had been mistaken by some of his failed employees for just another traveler—which was how he liked it. He was looking for people who could bring something unique and special to A'Qaban, and so far he'd been disappointed. Plus, he liked mingling with his people. It allowed him to feel the pulse of the country and test the mood of his fellow countrymen—that and the acuity of his staff.

En garde, Casey Michaels!

She was being watched. She could feel it like a ripple down her spine. Someone was stalking her; someone far more powerful than the officials she'd encountered so far was watching her. The constant warning signal in her head was making it hard to concentrate.

Impossible, Casey accepted with a gasp as she collided with a door.

* * *

Ouch! He grimaced as he watched Casey regroup and recover herself before moving on with the crowd heading for Immigration. At least she hadn't hurt herself, and the only thing stinging was her pride. Her cheeks had pinked up, but to her credit she showed no other outward sign of dismay. He moved ahead of her, always watching from an upper level. Casey worked for him, and therefore she was under his protection. This visit was a trial and as such it had to be fair. The other candidates had jumped through hoops and so would she, but he'd keep her safe as he'd kept them all safe—not that he'd watched any of the rest quite so avidly.

But that didn't mean he was going to step over the boundary of care into the dangerous territory of personal interest. It was just that Casey seemed to need more care than most. Other than that he was showing her the same courtesy he had extended to all of his employees.

Oh, really?

Had he felt like this when he'd first encountered the other candidates he would have had some serious concerns about his sexual orientation by now. And he had none.

She had researched the vast steel and glass structure that was A'Qaban International Airport on-line, but nothing could have prepared her for the sheer scale of the place. The glamour of gleaming crystal, bronze and glass, together with the cleanliness and the faint scent of something spicy on the air, was both exciting and distracting.

So no more walking into doors, Casey warned herself firmly—though it was easy to be sidetracked when she was basking in the husky Arabian language, the sound of robes fluttering and the pad of sandalled feet. Just the walk up to Immigration was an exotic introduction to the mysterious east, as the countless portraits of A'Qaban's *leader* were a heart-racing introduction to her boss.

There were images of the powerful young *leader* everywhere, and as Casey paused for a moment to take stock of one she realised it was the same official portrait they had back home, showing a magnificent figure clad in the traditional robes of a Bedouin warrior. She had never seen her boss in western clothes. She turned from that to inspect the royal standard, which was flying from a flagpole in the centre of the hall. A rich blue background hosted a silvery crescent moon, beneath which a rampant lion bared its teeth and roared a warning.

A shiver ran down Casey's spine as she remembered the lion was Sheikh Rafik's personal symbol. She had always thought it perfect for a man who had rowed for Eton, played rugby for Oxford, and boxed for the army during his time in the Special Forces, before stamping his authority on the business world as well as his country. Rafik al Rafar was the undisputed alpha lion of the Arabian Gulf—a man whose personal work ethic was famously merciless, and who expected nothing less of his team. A quiver of anticipation that had nothing to do with business ran through her at the prospect of meeting him.

Impressed by the efficiency of the airport staff, Casey was soon part of a fast-moving line in which she thought about her place in the Sheikh's organisation. Her passion for his country had no doubt helped her rise. Rebuilding A'Qaban was the most exciting project she could imagine. Bordered by a turquoise sea and framed by granite mountains, the country boasted a capital city to rival any in the world, and Casey was determined to see it become a market leader in the global tourist industry.

A'Qaban also had a priceless jewel—one that was largely un-discovered. In Casey's opinion its interior was the country's crowning glory. It was a wilderness largely untouched by man, other than the wandering Bedouin tribesmen, whom Sheikh Rafik al Rafar protected. Casey envisaged tours that respected the Bedouins' freedom to travel whilst celebrating their culture with carefully monitored wildlife safaris, ecological and educational trips, even archaeological digs to pique the interest of the world.

Her lips pressed down briefly with disappointment when she

remembered that she would be in the desert right now if the Sheikh hadn't changed his mind about her destination. There could be no other reason for her being dressed like an extra from the set of *Indiana Jones* and attracting more sideways glances than a stray camel. But if that was the only disappointment she had to cope with today…

Buoyed up with anticipation, she was just about to check her passport when her old friend intuition came knocking again. There *was* someone watching her. She had the strongest sense that a hunt was on and that she was the prey. But that was clearly the result of watching too many movies recently. The stack of DVDs back home fleshed out her non-existent personal life, and in the absence of romantic action kept her company at night.

As the line moved smoothly forward Casey took the sensation shimmering down her spine as a reminder to keep her wits about her. Her colleagues had warned her that Rafik al Rafar didn't play by the rules—a prospect that had excited her at the time, because she liked a challenge. But now she was here, in the middle of this trial by disorientation, she wasn't feeling quite so confident.

She shook off the feeling. She was determined to enjoy every moment of this trip—even the terminal building, which was decked out like the lobby of a six-star hotel. There were fountains to soothe the senses and cool the air, along with an abundance of lush green plants, and even indoor palm trees stretching their spiny fingers towards the twinkling glass ceiling.

It was just Casey Michaels who was feeling a little out of sorts, Casey accepted as she fought the feeling of being a very small speck of travelling dust in a busy, purposeful world. She was under no misapprehension. She was a piece on the Sheikh's chessboard, and if she didn't play the right move at the right time she would be swept out of the game.

A group of A'Qabani women distracted Casey as they fluttered past on silent feet, like so many graceful butterflies. As she smiled, kohl-lined eyes smiled back.

The A'Qabanis seemed such a friendly people. They made

her wish she could understand the secret language the women seemed to be transmitting from behind their silken veils. Their language hinted at a hidden world, and it was a world she longed to know more about. But, like the desert interior, that world would have to wait.

Casey passed through Immigration without incident, and at Customs was surprised to be waved on. It seemed strange to her that she, the most disreputable-looking person in the line, hadn't attracted so much as a challenge. But, heigh-ho, was she complaining? She had no desire to flaunt her stock of big knickers and sensible vests to a line of customs officials dressed in the immaculate robes and headdresses of A'Qaban.

Focusing on the exit signs, Casey quickened her pace. She didn't expect anyone to be waiting for her so her plan was to call a cab and ask to be taken to the nearest hotel. Once there, she would freshen up and contact the office.

She had barely made it halfway across the concourse when the crowd she was part of peeled away; moments after that she was surrounded by fearsome-looking guards. They wore a uniform of black tunics and baggy trousers, and they all had lethal daggers tucked into their belts. She turned full circle, but there was no escape.

The blood drained from Casey's face as dark, expressionless eyes confronted her. Nothing like this had ever happened to her before, and it was easily the most frightening experience of her life. What terrible sin had she unwittingly committed?

She didn't have to wait long to find out. The circle parted almost immediately to admit one man. *A hunk in jeans.*

Snug-fitting blue jeans, desert boots and a form-fitting top, to be precise. And that was before she took in the ruffled inky hair, sharp gaze, deep tan, sensual mouth and...*an earring?*

Casey's mind went into freefall. For a moment she couldn't think straight. The man was tall—threateningly so—and built like a kick boxer fresh from the ring. Swallowing deep, she called on all her powers of quick recovery. This was not the moment to be wrong-footed by the Sheikh.

'You move faster than I thought, Casey Michaels.'

Sheikh Rafik al Rafar's brown-black eyes were stunning, she registered shakily, stumbling into an awkward curtsey. *'Your Majesty—'*

'Leave your toadying at the door and call me Raffa.'

Raffa…

Raffa was not only the best-looking man she had seen in a long time—if ever—he had a voice that was honey-warm and barely accented, which strummed her senses in a way she had never experienced before. 'Raffa.'

'Ahlan wa sahlan, Casey Michaels…'

There was just the faintest touch of mockery in his voice. Could the bad-boy Sheikh tune in to her thoughts? She stared up into eyes that told a story Casey wasn't sure she was old enough to read, and her heart-rate soared when the ruler of A'Qaban touched his hand to his heart, his lips, and finally to his forehead.

'Ahlan wa sahlan beek, Your—er, Raffa.' She lowered her eyes, thanking her lucky stars that on joining a company owned by an Arab Sheikh she had learned the basics of his language. When she raised her head again it was to find the observant gaze licking over her with interest. Had she managed to buy herself a second chance?

'Come,' he said.

Come where? she wondered anxiously. Just so long as it wasn't the next flight home.

He took her to an office containing a desk and two uncomfortable-looking chairs, which was a relief. She walked in, while Raffa shut the door on the guards.

'What do you have in your backpack, Casey?' he asked, turning around.

For a moment she was completely thrown.

'Your backpack?' he prompted.

She put it down on the floor, leaning it against the utilitarian desk.

'Open it.'

Her cheeks fired up. Nature had granted Sheikh Rafik al Rafar a fierce, stubble-shaded face full of heart-stopping force and resolve. This was not your usual polished royal, but a hard man of the desert; there was no court of appeal here.

She opened the pack and straightened up. This was business, Casey reminded herself in an attempt to rebuild her flagging confidence. Business she could deal with; men were the problem. In business men were normal human beings, like anyone else, but when they stepped out of that box and became yang to her yin, that was something else. Plus, men as good-looking as this one never noticed her, let alone spoke to her. She'd had no practice dealing with someone so...

She was staring at Raffa's lips, Casey realised, jerking alert as he spoke.

'Just show me what you've got, Casey.'

CHAPTER TWO

'SHOW you what I've got?' Casey gulped as her mind reviewed the contents of her backpack. Raffa would hardly be impressed by her selection of giant-sized white cotton knickers.

'Take a seat, if you prefer,' he suggested, easing away from the wall.

And have him tower over her? 'I prefer to stand, if you don't mind.'

'As you wish.'

Oh, she did wish. And that was half the trouble. He only had to shrug to draw her attention to the width of his shoulders. She shrank back as he prowled closer.

'I just want to see how well you have prepared for the desert.'

His gaze was potent; his presence electrifying. He was toying with her, measuring her, pushing her to the limit in ways she had never been pushed before—and her body was really letting her down. This might be business, but she was acutely aware of Raffa and the hard masculine form beneath his casual clothes, and it was almost impossible not to think of the enormous bulge in the front of his jeans as a third presence in the room. Not that she should be thinking about it at all, of course.

And now tears were threatening. Casey Michaels—businesswoman printed through her like a stick of rock—was in serious danger of meltdown. Because if landing this job rested on her female attributes she might as well go home right now.

* * *

He had never done this before. He took it for granted that any executive working for him knew what they were doing. He had never plucked an employee hot from their flight and brought them to a private office to interrogate them before, and he had no excuse now. Except to say Casey Michaels intrigued him. He dreaded her turning out to be a vacuous blonde. He'd encountered his fair share over the years, and there was no place for them in his business.

As she pulled out the first object he realised with some amusement that she was anything but. The photo in Casey's personnel file was as misleading as his own official portrait. In fact, if she got the job, Casey's first task would be to put the presentation of company profiles out to tender.

She believed she had packed everything necessary, but had she? So much hung on this, Casey reflected tensely, pulling out her plastic sheet for collecting drinking water.

Raffa's lips pressed down with approval.

She held up her mirror, for signalling if she became lost…

The mirror garnered another nod.

Scissors, string and a fire stone for lighting tinder.

'Scissors?'

'Along with my Swiss army knife, my folding spade, and my water canister. They were packed in the hold in a waterproof zip-bag, which I have here—' She produced it.

Raffa indicated with a wave of his hand that she should continue.

A box of water-purifying tablets, six tubes of salt tablets, and an industrial-sized tub of insect repellent, along with a first-aid kit.

'And a map?' he pressed.

'Of course…' She produced the map, safely contained in a plastic cover to prevent it getting wet or ripped. 'And a compass.'

She was rewarded by the smallest tug of Raffa's lips.

'And the bulge?'

She dearly wanted to look at *his* bulge, but managed not to. 'My spare clothes.'

'A business suit?'

Not unless it was a grow-your-own-business suit, stowed in a water canister… 'Unfortunately, no.'

'Well, *fortunately*…' The word was laced with ironic emphasis '…we have shops here.'

A flood of heat rushed to Casey's face. 'If I'd known I was coming to the city I would have packed differently.' She froze. Judging by the expression on Raffa's face, no one ever interrupted him. Which raised another problem. Reining herself in she could do. Changing her personality completely in the short time available was going to prove a little more difficult.

Raffa's powerful shoulders eased in a shrug. 'I wanted you here,' he said, as if that were the only explanation necessary. But it was not the end of her frustration. Raffa was just so aggravatingly nonchalant, while she was…

So out of her depth in his presence?

It wasn't her business sense letting her down now, but the tension crackling between them.

'You can pack everything away,' Raffa said, providing her with a welcome distraction. 'I'm satisfied you are as prepared as you could be for the desert…'

Inwardly, she cheered. Thank goodness he hadn't asked her to dig any deeper and reveal the six sets of sensible underwear, the rape alarm, and the condoms her ever-practical if misguided mother had insisted she must pack.

He brooded as he watched Casey pack away her belongings. Her qualifications were good on paper, her work ethic unquestioned, but he needed more than that. The person who would eventually lead his marketing team must show total commitment to A'Qaban, and be a questing, innovative, initiative-seizing individual, capable of working solo and producing results without requiring constant monitoring or supervision.

His gaze swept over Casey again. Her outfit was outlandish, almost comical, but somehow she managed to pull it off. The combination of naivety and absolute determination gave her an unaffected charm—though he suspected she could be stubborn, given half a chance.

He'd take that as a plus, he decided, though she would have to be prepared to travel as and when required, and adapt to changing itineraries if necessary. She would also have to cope with the interior. He'd had the last candidate airlifted out when they couldn't hack it, and until he was sure of Casey she was staying in the city.

The question was, could she cope with anything more rigorous than a sanitised desert kingdom? He was quite keen to find out, and found himself silently urging her on.

Come on, Casey Michaels, show me what you've got...

She was tired from the travelling and shaken up by the speed of events. And by Rafik al Rafar

By him mostly.

She held him entirely responsible.

She could even identify, with a nose well trained at the perfume counter of countless department stores, each ingredient in his exotic cologne: vanilla—an aphrodisiac, sandalwood—a sultry spice, and—

'Shall we go?' he prompted. 'Casey?' Dipping his head, he gave her a disturbingly direct stare. 'I'm going to take you to your hotel to drop your bag,' he said, 'and then—'

Her face flamed red with embarrassment. She was twenty-five years old and didn't possess a single atom of know-how when it came to men.

'Then I'll buy you a suit,' he said, rather disappointingly.

'You don't need to. I—'

'Never accept gifts from men?' He raised one sweeping brow.

'I've got money with me.'

He shrugged. 'If you prefer to pay, that's okay with me.'

She was still staring into his eyes like an obedient puppy, Casey realized—something it was all too easy to do.

Holding the door, Raffa was waiting for her. 'Let's go,' he said.

She nodded, not trusting herself to speak.

Raffa paused just in front of the main exit doors leading from the concourse. His guards, anticipating this, stopped instantly and stood to attention.

'Welcome to A'Qaban,' he said to Casey. 'My country is your country for the next few days.'

Heat was sweeping over her in waves. It had nothing to do with the brilliant sunshine. She felt so grubby and travel-stained compared to Raffa, who was coolness personified. His gaze was measured as he looked at her, and faintly amused. She felt under a scrutiny from which she suspected there would be no let-up while she was in A'Qaban. It was impossible not to feel honoured by the pledge he'd just made her, and also impossible not to feel very much threatened on the personal front. It was as if her very womanhood was on the line. It shouldn't matter to her if that was found wanting just so long as she landed this job—but it did matter; it mattered far more than it should have done.

He gestured towards the limousine that had pulled up at the curb. 'Let me take your backpack for you.'

'That's very kind of you.'

'I don't do kind.'

Blunt words that for some reason made her quiver all over.

Raffa's fierce fighting men had formed a private corridor in order for them to make the short transit from the airport doors to the royal vehicle. It had blacked out windows—a hermetically sealed chamber lined in softest kidskin, where she would be shut off from the world.

Panicking, she held back. Overheating, she dragged off her unbecoming hat.

'You should wait until you are under cover,' Raffa warned as she shook out her hair. 'The sun is deceptively strong. While you are in A'Qaban you must take every opportunity to avoid the heat.'

But the heat was all in his eyes.

CHAPTER THREE

HE FELT Casey next to him on the seat of the limousine like a lick of flame on a heart turned cold. So many women; so few memories—or at least none he cared to keep. Perhaps that was why he was so cynical. He had planned to turn around his country in the same way he'd turn around a business—with balance sheets, boardroom battles and cold, hard fact. The possibility that there might be something missing from that scheme had never occurred to him before Casey Michaels arrived on the scene. Now he wondered if her take on things might refresh the ideas he'd had. But he would never find out while she was tense like this.

He settled back, hoping that would reassure her. She sat stiffly for a while and then turned away from him to stare out of the window. He inhaled her fragrance. Light and floral, it counter-balanced his musk and spice perfectly. The contrast suggested to him that it might be time to recruit someone different from the hardbitten, results-driven individuals he usually selected. But was Casey right for A'Qaban?

As he watched her toying with her soft blonde curls, winding them round and round her slender fingers, he told himself not to be so ridiculous. A woman like Casey Michaels could never be up to the job on offer, and only his libido suggested otherwise.

'Are those Artesian wells?'

He leaned closer, surprised and pleased by her interest. 'Yes, that's right...'

He drew back slowly, wondering if she had felt his heat as he had felt hers. He was conscious of how pale her skin was. Dusted with freckles, it had the bloom of a peach…and the scent of a woman. She would burn in the sun, he realised; yet another reason to send her home. But another, darker side of him yearned to taste her, to see her eyes burn with passion and lust for him. It was all too easy to imagine making love to Casey until she fell asleep in his arms.

'Oh, look!' she exclaimed, distracting him. 'A camel.'

'Really?' Imagine that. A camel in the desert. Her childish excitement only underscored the decision he had already made. She must go home.

'I can't believe the desert comes right up to the margins of the highway,' she said, turning to him with luminous appeal in her clear blue eyes.

There was such innocence in those eyes, and at the very moment when he should have withdrawn from it he responded. 'If you look to towards the mountains you'll be able to see more camels on the horizon.'

'Oh, yes!' she exclaimed, breathless with excitement as the black silhouettes of the marching dromedaries appeared framed in gold against the darkening sky.

She was practically pressing her face to the car window in her enthusiasm, all thoughts of nervousness in his presence forgotten. And when she held her fine-boned hands to her face and exclaimed in wonder it was the strongest warning yet to book her flight home. He shouldn't feel moved like this. This was business.

And his decision might have remained that straightforward had not the delicate column of her neck led to such a stubborn chin. For all her lack of worldliness, he suspected there was more to Casey Michaels than met the eye. He switched his thoughts from bed to business. She wouldn't be moulded as easily as some of the other candidates. She would have her own opinions and her own fresh take on ideas. She might even have some innovative suggestions to add to the pot. Could he afford to deny A'Qaban a new young talent because he didn't trust himself not to take her to bed?

'I think this is very exciting,' she said, spinning round to speak to him. 'And I can't wait to get started. It's such a challenge.'

She made the challenge sound like a supreme prize—much as he felt about it himself. He confined himself to an acknowledging dip of the head. The lust Casey had inspired in him suggested the next couple of days would be a challenge for both of them—if only because this was not a woman to take and enjoy, or a woman who would understand that a man in his position had nothing more to offer her beyond a few nights of passion; this was a woman instinct told him should be treasured and valued for her originality. With Casey's innocence standing between them, for now he had to admit he was facing stalemate.

Raffa made it easy for her to forget she was sitting next to a *king*, though forgetting the charisma of the man was rather more difficult. His warm, spicy scent embraced every part of her until she tingled. Just because she shied away from men it didn't mean she was incapable of feeling, and with Raffa's unbelievable levels of testosterone buzzing in the air she was feeling rather too much of everything.

He appeared to be relaxed and unaware of her interest, so she took the opportunity to steal a glance at him. A man all at ease, he sprawled on the seat with his hair ruffled and his pirate earring glinting in the slanting rays of the dying sun. He was just so cool and sexy, with eyes full of promise and a mouth shaped for fantasy kisses. Why did he have to be her boss? She guessed it was some time since he had shaved, because his stubble was thicker, blacker, sharper than she had ever seen on any man.

Would it hurt to have that stubble rasp against, say, the tender skin on her neck, her cheek…her breast? She shivered at the thought of it. She only had a few bungled kisses to go on, and they had practically put her off kissing for life. Usually overly moist, they had convinced her she wasn't missing much. But she imagined Raffa's kisses would be different. He would be an accomplished kisser, as in all else. She flinched away when his lips curved as their gazes clashed. Had he read her thoughts? Sensed her fascination? If he had read something into it...

She had to calm herself with steady breathing. Turning away to stare out of the heavily tinted windows only increased the impression that she was entering the mysterious, closed world she had glimpsed at the airport. And, yes, she was eager to learn what lay behind the silken veil, but would she be permitted to look? Or would she be taken from one sterile, air-conditioned capsule to the next without ever once experiencing the real A'Qaban?

She had to fight for the opportunity to see the country if she had any hope of selling A'Qaban to the world, Casey realised. But if *he* took her behind the silken curtain, what then?

Her insides melted at the thought of it, and sensation pooled between her thighs. She wanted him to take her there. She wanted him to touch her *there*...tenderly and persuasively— and, yes, persistently, rhythmically, stroking until she'd had enough. He'd ease her thighs wide apart and cup her buttocks to keep her in the most receptive position—and of course he'd pay close attention to her responses and stop the moment she wanted him to—

'Not too hot, are you?' Raffa said, turning as she sighed.

'No, I'm fine,' she fudged, pretending to ease cramped limbs, though goodness knew there was enough room in the limousine to stretch out.

Her imagination would get her into trouble one day, Casey acknowledged, but while her fertile mind insisted on teasing her with erotic possibilities in A'Qaban, her sensible self knew there was no law that said she had to open those doors and walk through.

Maybe not. But she did have to shift position discreetly now and then to ease the worrying signs of arousal those thoughts had provoked.

* * *

By the time they turned into the flag-lined drive of what Raffa briefly explained was A'Qaban's premier hotel, Casey realised the towering pink stone building, modelled on the lines of an ancient fort, was something else she would be expected to market. She paid close attention. If the inside of the building were only half as impressive as the outside the hotel would sell itself, and the truth was she ached to take on tougher projects. Surely it was the diversity of culture and landscape that would sell A'Qaban to the world? She *had* to win the right to visit the desert.

As the chauffeur drew the limousine to a halt at the foot of a wide sweep of steps, and Casey saw doormen better dressed than she was, she knew what her first steps towards that goal must be.

But Raffa spoke first. 'Take some rest,' he said abruptly.

Maybe he couldn't wait to get rid of her.

'You'll be working flat out tomorrow. You'll find a list of essential telephone numbers in your room.'

So he had changed his mind about the shopping trip. 'And my business suit?'

'I'll call an aide and have a selection sent up to your suite.'

Casey frowned. So some man was going to assume he knew what she should be wearing? 'That won't be necessary, thank you,' she said firmly. 'I'll make my own arrangements.'

'That is the way we do things here.'

'Well, it's not my way to have someone choose my clothes.' She had intended to couch her refusal in a way she hoped Raffa would not find offensive, but unfortunately it didn't come out that way, and she found herself confronting his narrowed gaze. 'I'm used to picking out and paying for my clothes myself, you see,' she added, hoping to soften the effect of her first sally.

Had she gone too far?

Raffa's stern expression exhibited surprise, and then faint amusement.

Which left her with just one thing to sort out. 'When will I see you again?'

'I'll be in touch.' He turned away, effectively dismissing her.

She had gone way too far.

Plus, as he turned to leave her she got the distinct and very embarrassing impression that he had not thought she was talking about their next business meeting. 'I mean when will our next business meeting be?' she clarified.

'What else?' Leaning half in and half out of the car, Raffa spoke to her in a muted and discreet tone that allowed him to get his message across loud and clear: 'If this doesn't work out for you, Casey, there are plenty of other jobs in my organization.'

Roger that. 'But this is the job I want,' she said stubbornly, holding his gaze for as long as she dared so there could be no mistake.

Sweeping inky brows rose minutely. Shutting the car door, Raffa made some signal, and then both he and the limousine swept away.

So she liked to live dangerously, he mused, turning to watch Casey walk up the steps of the hotel. It amused him to see that she had managed to wrestle her backpack from the horrified doorman already. She was quite determined to go it alone and she made him smile. She hadn't given him so much as a chance to have the shopping mall closed for her to have a spending spree on him. Oh, no, that wasn't Casey Michaels's way.

He eased back in his seat, but found it impossible to relax. He swung round in his seat to take one final look at her.

In fact…

'Turn around, please,' he told the driver. 'We're going back.'

Oh, wow! She really must stop running around the suite, picking things up and putting them down again, and try to get over the fact that she had been given accommodation that exceeded her wildest dreams by her wildest dreams.

Racing into the bathroom, she turned on the drench shower,

getting drenched in the process, before sprinting back into the biggest bedroom she'd ever seen.

Who needed a gym when you had your own running track?

And, no, her backpack wasn't in here, it was still in the ballroom-sized lounge, Casey remembered, chasing back the way she'd come. She had the whole of the top floor to herself, for goodness' sake. It was less a penthouse and more a country. Even her bulging pack looked like a doll's accessory, lying where she had discarded it on the football-pitch-sized rug in the centre of the floor.

Fighting with the buckles, she flung it open and delved inside. The best she could come up with was a white T-shirt, a pair of old jeans and some flip-flops, but at least they were clean and fresh, and they'd have to do. Flinging the chosen outfit onto a chair, she raced back to the bathroom, tugging off clothes as she ran. Stepping gratefully beneath the tepid water, she soaped herself down. This was a bathroom fit for a king—a bathroom the size of her family home—a bathroom lined in pink-veined cream marble with a matching floor. There were black granite surfaces and golden taps. It wasn't to her taste, but there was no doubt it was the height of luxury, the height of decadence, the height of—well, the height. And there was even a store-sized selection of high end products for her to choose from.

But no time to use them.

She grabbed for towels in her excitement, plucking the first ones that came to hand from the heated rail. Wrapping her hair in one, she almost managed to wrap her body in the other before barging through the door, and—

Paling with shock, she remained rooted to the spot, clutching her wholly inadequate towel over those bits most obviously reacting to the *ruler* of A'Qaban.

Raffa was currently lounging on the sofa. Surprised, excited and embarrassed, she performed a virginal two-step, backing her way to the bathroom door, conscious all the while her towel was slipping. 'Wh…who let you in?'

'Your butler.'

'My...?' She didn't even know she *had* a butler. How many more invisible men were sharing the penthouse with her?

Unfolding his powerful frame, Raffa straightened up and did the last thing she expected. 'What are you doing?' She backed away nervously as he strolled towards her.

'I thought you might need these...'

He sounded so relaxed she wondered if dealing with half-naked employees was par for the course. But then she saw what he was holding. As Raffa's cool, sexy gaze remained steady on her face, she extended one hand cautiously to take the jeans and top she'd chosen to wear.

'Most people who stay here use this space as a meeting room and reception area,' he explained.

And don't run around it naked, Casey gathered, pressing back against the bathroom door. 'Could you...?' How to make the required gesture without dropping her towel?

Fortunately, Raffa anticipated her. 'Could I turn around?' he suggested.

Could he read her mind? She hoped not. 'Please...'

'My pleasure...'

It was a relief to turn his back on Casey and allow his stern expression to unbend a little. She was so warm and pink and flustered; she was adorable. Not a quality he sought, necessarily, in his executives.

'Okay, you can turn round now.'

How piquant to be given permission. But there had been too many compliant milksops in his life recently, and he rated ladies who stood up to him. *Executives* who stood up to him, he amended.

'Did you need something?' Casey sounded concerned, professional, as she straightened her clothes.

'The shopping trip,' he reminded her.

'I've got it covered.'

'You have?' He narrowed his eyes, viewing the towel she had

discarded on the floor. She blushed violently as she explained, 'I called a cab.'

'No need.'

'No need?'

As she angled her face and stared at him with an ingenuous look in her clear blue eyes he got a jolt. She affected him in a way no executive should. That didn't stop him sticking to his plan. 'I'll take you.'

'You?'

She looked alarmed, as if he had suggested something immoral. His gaze dropped from her eyes to her lips. They were full, moist, and slightly parted. He had certainly never wanted to kiss one of his executives before.

'Why?' she said suspiciously.

Had he had been expecting wall-to-wall gratitude? 'Because it's the least I can do,' he explained. 'I brought you here with a backpack and a shovel, and you need a suit.' He made a gesture, as if to say that was an end of it. 'Shall we go?' He looked towards the door.

'Only if you promise I can pay.'

'What?' As he held her gaze he was amused to think anyone could be so humdrum on paper and yet so original in the flesh.

She brandished her purse. 'Promise me…'

'I thought Sheikhs were supposed to pay?' He spoke lightly to restore her mood, but she only blushed again and looked away. He guessed she was concerned she had overstepped the mark and had lost the job without a hand being played. What would the papers have to say about this? he wondered as he gave his word.

'Thank you. And as for Sheikhs,' she admitted shyly, 'I really don't know—you're my first.'

And your last, he thought fiercely.

'*Muta assif,* Casey Michaels,' he intoned in a deceptively calm voice. 'Please accept my apologies if I have insulted you.'

'No insult,' she hurried to assure him. 'It's just that I'm used to paying my own way.'

'You should never apologise for that.' He held the door for her.

CHAPTER FOUR

THE limousine had gone home to bed, and in its place was a blood red Lamborghini.

'You wanted to go shopping didn't you?' Raffa prompted, when Casey remained rooted to the spot, staring at the fabulous vehicle in confusion.

'Of course I do, but—'

'But what?'

But it was a small car where they'd almost be touching—where they'd be sharing the same air, the same breath. 'Is the boot big enough?'

'For one business suit?' Raffa looked at her sideways.

What to say? She couldn't admit that she didn't trust herself to sit so close to him without her brain scrambling and something addled coming out of her mouth.

'The shops don't stay open all night.'

She took the prompt as a warning to get a move on, and made her way to the open door where, with as much grace as she could muster, she performed the contortions required to insert a reasonably well-upholstered body into a letter-box-sized opening.

'It's a moulded seat,' Raffa explained helpfully as she bumped her hips in a dozen different places.

Moulded around Tinkerbell's bottom, Casey presumed, forcing her own rather more ample curves into the available space. 'Lovely…' She beamed, remembering not to flinch as Raffa settled himself beside her.

He was being helpful, she reminded herself. He didn't need to do this.

And she didn't need to stare at his strong, capable hands on the wheel, or his legs…But she could see the muscles in his thighs working as he operated the vehicle, and they were really gripping her attention. She raised her chin in time to see Raffa lower what to her would be around a month's worth of wages in designer sunglasses past the obstacle of his ridiculously long eyelashes and part-way down his nose. Far too late now to evade his laser stare.

'It is a very big shopping mall. Give me a clue as to what you need and I'll decide where to park up.'

'Just a serviceable suit.'

'Which you'll wear with flip-flops? Don't waste my time,' he warned, settling his sunglasses into position. 'Remember the five "P's".'

'The five what?' She turned to look at him in bewilderment.

'Proper Preparation Prevents Poor Performance.'

'Of course…' *What?* 'I won't,' she assured him.

As Raffa gunned the engine and released the brake her full attention returned to his face. He hated shopping; she could understand that—he was a man. But maybe, just maybe, she could use this opportunity to turn the shopping trip into an advantage…'I can't wait to get star—'

The rest of Casey's sentence was lost in the roar of the colossal engine as the Lamborghini took off. G-Force knocked her back in her seat, rendering conversation impossible.

He would give Casey the same chance he'd given all the other candidates.

And then…?

She'd fail, and he'd send her home, of course.

His lips tugged as his body argued with this sombre inner

counsel. It would be interesting to see which half of him won through in the end.

He drew into the extensive car park, where a valet was waiting to park the car. 'Money?' he prompted, before Casey got out. He was still prepared to help her, but she had plumbed the pockets of her jeans, coming up with a handful of screwed-up notes and some spare change, which she now showed him. He stared at it dubiously. 'Are you sure that's enough?'

'It's plenty for what I need,' she told him, jutting out her chin. 'It's more than I usually spend…'

He raised a brow and said nothing.

He followed her inside as his silent guards peeled out of the following cars. This was a first for them, he mused as he left the order of the car park behind for the bustle and glamour of an up-market mall. He motioned his guards to remain in the background as Casey consulted the mall guide. Having looked around to get her bearings, she headed off.

He followed her with interest. Shopping malls in A'Qaban were for exclusive labels only. Most of the shops didn't reveal anything so vulgar as the cost of an article, and though personally he hated floating prices, with increasing wealth they had become a fact of life in the country. The general consensus was, if you had to ask the price, chances were you couldn't afford it. To him that was not only insulting, but open to misuse, allowing prices to be thought up on a whim. It was on his list of things to change—but not today, because this was Casey Michaels's day and his concerns were all for her.

He had brought Casey to A'Qaban to test her business acumen, not to humiliate her, he reminded himself, staying right behind her. If it got anywhere close to that, he'd step in.

He waited in the shadows of the first boutique to see how she got on. The shop specialised in clothes he thought far too old for her. As he had feared, the misnamed 'assistants' were dismissive of Casey, and barely looked her way as she searched the rails. He felt insulted and angry on her behalf. He wasn't surprised to see a photograph of the late Sheikh, a distant relative of his, still hanging on the wall. Attitudes here were still in the Dark Ages. He intended A'Qaban to be a country of equal opportunity, where everyone would be treated with respect. The employees here had some shocks in store when that happened, but for now Casey was stuck with the ancient regime, and it pained him to see her embarrassment when she came out of the shop.

'I'm sorry to keep you, Raffa, but there's nothing I like in here.'

'Don't apologise.' Seeing her face fall, and knowing she couldn't afford anything in the shop, he nudged Casey into the shadows, where no one could see what they were doing.

She turned her face up to him, staring at him warily.

'Call it an advance on your wages,' he murmured, wanting to save her pride.

'No…Please…'

Her tiny hand pushed his away as he tried in vain to pass a wad of banknotes to her.

'I mean it, Raffa. Please don't…'

He eased back, respecting her position, and had to satisfy himself with a raised brow at the snooty manageress as they left the shop.

Seeing his face clearly in the light, the woman blenched.

Without a word of complaint Casey headed for the next shop, but when she was shown the same lack of attention he decided he must put her out of her misery.

'No, really—I've learned a lot,' she explained when he again drew her to one side.

Such as she couldn't afford anything in A'Qaban? Such as people without enough money got snubbed here? That wasn't what he wanted for his country. He felt ashamed, and was already reaching for his wallet again when Casey's face suddenly lit up.

'Ah, that's what I need,' she exclaimed, heading off in the direction of a well-stocked stationery shop.

'Don't get distracted,' he warned. He was sympathetic, but he'd brought her here for a purpose, not for a protracted shopping trip.

'Will you wait outside for me?'

He ground his jaw. He could understand she wouldn't want him witnessing any more embarrassing situations, but now was not the time to be searching for a postcard home. 'Will you please take some money from me and get whatever it is you need?'

'I won't need a lot of money for this,' she informed him.

Intrigued, he followed her into the shop, where she bought a clipboard and a pen. 'That's it?' he said as she paid for them.

'What more do I need?'

'Do you intend wearing them?' he asked dryly.

Casey's response was to press back against the counter, clutching her purchases to her breast like a shield.

'That was a joke?' he prompted lightly.

'Of course I don't intend wearing them.'

She acted bold, but not for the first time he sensed her fear of him as a man. It was raw and very real to her, and it made him curious, but for now he stepped away. The last thing on his mind was to intimidate her.

'Will you come with me?' she said, as if concerned she'd tried his patience too far.

'Lead the way…' He made a gesture for her to go first, noticing her lips were parted and her gaze was fixed on him. And she was breathing too fast. She was a lot more innocent than he could ever have imagined, but she *was* aroused.

She was vulnerable, he told himself sternly as she walked past, and as such Casey Michaels was untouchable.

He matched his stride to her shorter one, keen to see where this was going. He waved his guards away when they threatened to get in her way. She was retracing her steps, he noticed with interest, heading back to the first shop. He waited while she went inside. He waited with rather less forbearance when the same snooty assistants were rude to her again. They ignored her. Or at least they ignored her for the first five minutes—after which they paid her a lot more attention. Perhaps that had something to do with the fact that Casey had taken up a position in the centre of their store and was using her clipboard to write down what appeared to be a detailed inventory of their stock.

'Can I help you?' the assistant detailed to apprehend Casey demanded.

'No, thank you,' Casey replied politely. 'But I'm pretty sure I can help you.'

Botoxed brows rose as far as they were able.

His ears pricked up. He took a step forward and had to curb his impatience to step in. If the woman saw him, whatever project Casey had embarked on would be sunk.

'Actually,' Casey continued in the same pleasant and confiding tone, 'I'm conducting a survey for Sheikh Rafik al Rafar bin Haktari on the level of service customers receive in his stores.' As the woman tensed, she added, 'The Sheikh *does* own this boutique, I believe?'

'Together with every other shop in the mall,' the assistant confirmed, in a voice that not only lacked its former sneer but had gained a wobble.

'Yes, that's what I thought,' Casey agreed. 'You see, I am what's known in the trade as a Secret Shopper.'

At this point he thought the assistant in more need of assistance than Casey, and had to admit he was impressed by the end result—which involved Casey making a clean sweep of the store without a penny changing hands.

'Sale or approval,' she explained to him breezily on her way out.

He got it now. He would pay for them eventually. Clever? Yes. But ultimately disappointing. It always came down to money in the end. He could only hope that if Casey intended to repeat the exercise she would choose a younger range of clothes for her next rapacious fashion trolley-dash.

But she had another surprise in store for him.

'I shan't keep them,' she confided as they strode together down the brilliantly lit mall.

'So what will you do with them?' He waved a hovering security guard forward to take the packages.

'Return them, of course.'

'But how does that help your situation?'

She gave him a look, clearly getting into her stride now. 'Can I have a little longer to prove my point?'

'As long as there is a point to prove, you can take as long as you like—within reason.'

Her next stop was a cashpoint machine. Instinctively, he checked around for paparazzi. Sheikh Rafik al Rafar, billionaire tycoon, waiting patiently beside a cashpoint while his companion *du jour* extracted a measly two hundred dollars—counting it carefully before stowing it safely in her purse—that would make a great headline.

'That should be enough,' she said, glancing up at him.

Wisely, he declined to comment, and merely indicated that Casey should lead the way.

The moment he saw her destination he understood. There was one store of international renown that had managed to transcend labels and had acquired a cachet of its own. It had done this by being a fast follower of the catwalk fashions at a fraction of the cost. And it was to this store that Casey took him now. She bought a small selection of clothes, with a pretty shawl to wear over them, the cheapest of bags, and a cardigan.

'I expect you'd prefer me to cover my arms in some situations,' she observed thoughtfully.

Actually, he'd like her to uncover everything, and he only pulled back from those thoughts because some better part of him conceded she was too pure for him to sully. Such a pity—so much unlit fire going to waste in her veins.

She had bought a pair of trousers too, and he had to admit that pleased him. If she did survive the interview in the city there were still those traditionalists in the interior who looked down on shows of flesh, and he didn't want anyone looking down on Casey Michaels. Other than him, of course, and then only from his height advantage, he reflected wryly as she unfurled her tiny hand to show him the coins she had left.

'And I've still got change,' she told him triumphantly.

'You've done well,' he admitted, 'but you should have let me pay.'

'Why?' Her blue eyes levelled on his.

'Non-taxable expenses?' he teased her, deadpan.

'You draw expenses?' she challenged him. No soon had she spoken than she slapped a hand over her mouth, exclaiming how sorry she was, and that it was no business of hers whether or not he paid tax to himself.

'What am I going to do with you?' He really meant it. But, concluding tiredness had finally caught up with her, and that she was probably dehydrated too, he decided on a change of plan.

'Juice?' Her voice was trembling. 'Oh, yes, please—I'm just dying for a drink.'

'Save that sentiment for the desert.'

She was instantly alert, clearly not so tired as he had thought her. They both knew the promise of a visit to the desert meant she was still in the game. How could she not be? he thought, when he saw her eyes darken.

She shouldn't undercut him when he spoke. She mustn't walk too close to him, either. Or assume anything, Casey reprimanded herself as Raffa led the way towards a chi-chi café in the basement of the mall. An opportunity to visit the desert *and* keep in the running for this job hung by a thread, and so it was more important than ever to show the best of her professional self. She must be all about business from this moment on.

But how easy was that when nothing compared to wanting Raffa in all the wrong ways…ways that had nothing to do with business at all?

* * *

The combination of apple, mint and celery in the smoothie was delicious, and so was the sight of Casey's full red lips pursing around the straw.

'Some time during my stay,' she said, biting her lip as she thought out loud, 'I'd like to come back to this mall.'

'To do what?' he said suspiciously.

'To conduct a proper survey.'

'Go on,' he pressed.

'Well, it seems to me that some of these stores are hardly welcoming…'

Understatement, he reflected.

'And if you're serious about increasing footfall significantly as the tourist industry grows, I think your staff would benefit from more training. It would both incentivise them and increase your profits substantially.'

He was leaning forward, staring into her eyes, finding it harder and harder to remember why it was so important to keep this on a professional footing. 'You don't say?' he mocked gently.

'But I do say,' she assured him, all confidence and reason in her role of marketing executive. 'Some of us might not be as rich as others, but our money is just as good. And if lots of us little people spend—'

'Little people?' In spite of his best efforts, his lips curved. Nothing on earth would convince him to think of Casey as little or insignificant in any way—or, indeed, others like her. Since when had wealth become a measure of the man? 'It has never been my intention to build an exclusive enclave in A'Qaban, solely for the rich to enjoy.'

'Then why don't you make use of my expertise in not having lots of money while you can?' she suggested playfully.

'I might just do that.'

Her eyes flashed, and then she remembered who he was and looked down. He liked the way she grew in confidence whenever business was under discussion, but would she ever achieve that same degree of poise in her personal life? He hoped so—though perhaps not while she was here in A'Qaban. He could do many things, but he hadn't yet learned how to rein in his libido, and she could feel it however hard he tried to curb his interest.

She drained her drink and, with all talk of business over between them, she seemed at a loss again. She flicked him a glance and looked away. As one blush started bleeding into another he felt he must reassure her.

'You're doing okay.' Reaching out, he briefly covered her hand with his.

'I'm fine,' she assured him, flinching back. And then, gaining in confidence, she added, 'I'm not relying on instinct. I have a degree in—'

'Shopping?' he suggested dryly.

'In retail marketing,' she corrected him solemnly.

He liked that. No one pulled him up—ever. He liked it almost more than when she blushed and looked away. He liked it too much, he decided, standing up.

'Shall we go?' He held her chair for her, discreetly waving away the bodyguards who would have done that for him. 'And now I'm taking you straight back to the hotel,' he insisted, his gaze drawn to the dark circles beneath her eyes. 'You look tired.'

'It's only temporary. I'll be up bright and early in the morning,' she assured him.

She'd sleep comfortably through to noon, he guessed as their gazes briefly met and held. He wanted to give her the morning off, but how would that be fair to the other candidates? And now, before the image of Casey curled up and warm in bed could take hold of him, he made a move. 'Come on, let's go,' he insisted, eager to break the spell she had woven.

'Thank you for the smoothie,' she said, shifting awkwardly in front of him. 'And for…'

'For what?' he prompted when she hesitated.

'For giving me this chance.'

'You earned this chance,' he told her steadily.

'I know you have some weeding out to do—'

'Stop fishing,' he warned. 'You'll get my verdict like everyone else—before you leave.'

Distress flared in her eyes and was just as quickly gone. He'd make no allowances for Casey forming some emotional attachment to A'Qaban. What he'd told her was how it had to be. He wanted the best candidate for the job, and she'd be treated exactly the same as all the other candidates.

'Is a suit all right for tomorrow morning?' she asked in a much more businesslike fashion when he dropped her at the hotel.

Nude would have been his choice, if the circumstances had been different. 'A suit is good,' he agreed, passing her bags to the doorman. 'Or smart casual would be fine too.'

They shook hands formally. He resisted the temptation to convey anything at all in his eyes, but when he stared back at her through the rearview mirror of the Lamborghini his foot stamped down on the throttle as if he couldn't quite believe the effect she'd had on him.

CHAPTER FIVE

CASEY didn't go straight to bed, as Raffa had suggested, but stayed up analysing the small amount of data she had managed to collect at the shopping mall. She even went down to the hotel business centre and typed it up. She wanted to impress him. It was important to her. Suddenly this wasn't about the job any more, but about Raffa seeing her potential as an effective co-worker. She wasn't the blunderer who had arrived all hot and bothered in A'Qaban, but to prove that to him she had to make sure everything she suggested in the way of change placed A'Qaban above criticism. Integrity was everything if she was going to build a world-class brand.

And she *was* going to build a world-class brand.

She put her computer to bed in the early hours, took a bath to ease feet screaming from pounding acres of marble mall floor, and tried to sleep. She couldn't. Her brain was racing. Getting out of bed, she slipped on a robe and, picking up the previous day's newspaper, unfurled the business pages of the *A'Qaban Times*.

What an eye-opener that was. The first headline to catch her attention read:

Car numberplate fetches $3 million in charity auction! 'Father gave me blank cheque to buy new licence plates for my 4-wheel drive,' reports young socialite.

Holy moley! Dropping the newspaper on the bed, she paced the room, trying to picture that amount of money piled up in stacks around its perimeter. If it were piled up next to the off-roader it would probably hide it from view. But if the thought of so much excess went against her grain, at least it was a consolation to think a charity would benefit. And she mustn't lose sight of her primary objective, which was to secure the job of marketing a country. So forget about blank cheques, car numberplates and over-indulged minor celebrities…

And Raffa.

Or she'd never get to sleep.

But as she wearily pulled back the bedcovers she couldn't forget any of it; especially Raffa…

She must have drifted off to sleep some time in the early hours, Casey realized, as she woke slowly to find dawn peeping through the shutters. Making happy sounds of contentment, she decided to treat herself to another hour in bed. Firm and big, the bed was dressed with crisp white sheets that carried the faint scent of jasmine, and, like the hotel Raffa had put her up in, it was divine. Thankfully, the butler had remained invisible—ergo, also divine. And sleep was divine, Casey concluded, stretching lazily before turning her face into the soft bank of pillows. There was even a divine telephone within reach of the bed…

A ringing telephone.

She groped for it, grimacing at the unwelcome intrusion. '…llo…?'

'Ten minutes. Downstairs in the lobby.'

Raffa!

She sat bolt-upright.

The line was dead before she had chance to reply.

Rolling out of bed, she landed on the floor. Picking herself up, she staggered, half asleep, in the general direction of the bathroom, blundering into things as she went. She managed to run up a total of stubbed toe, banged head and almost dislocated shoulder. Raffa had made it sound cheerfully like the middle of the day. And why not, when he had probably worked out and swum a thousand metres before showering down and placing his call?

After which thought, she entered the bathroom and turned the shower to its lowest temperature. Readying herself, she leaped in. And leaped out again, shrieking. There was only so much she could cope with at five o' clock in the morning.

Teeth chattering, she set the shower to warm and returned. Washing her hair, she soaped down quickly, rinsed off again, and stepped out.

Better.

Much better.

Wrapping a towel around her head, she cleaned her teeth, sprayed deodorant everywhere—it stung in some places—and gargled with mouthwash.

Okay, she was most definitely awake now.

Scampering into the bedroom, she pounced on her knapsack and plucked out her sensible knickers. Teaming those with her sensible bra the one that didn't show beneath the shirt she'd bought, she chose dark trousers and a red cardigan rather than a jacket.

High heels, of course…

With trousers?

Discarding the trousers, she tugged on the skirt.

No good. Pale legs.

Throwing it off, she grabbed the trousers again.

Shirt, trousers, high heels…

Shirt, trousers, desert boots…

Definitely high heels.

Spinning in front of the full-length mirror, she viewed herself as critically as a two-and-a-half-second spin would allow.

Whatever the day ahead held, she was ready for it.

There was no time for make-up, and her hair was a candy-floss explosion she just bound in a band as she raced to the door.

Her hand stalled halfway to the handle. Back up. What about the survey she'd prepared?

And some of the duty free scent she'd bought on the plane. Squirt everywhere; sneeze. Finished.

Ready.

Two seconds to tuck the survey under her arm in a professional manner, and tip her chin at a businesslike angle. And still two minutes left on the ten-minute deadline.

She opened the door. 'Oh, hell!'

'Hello, yourself…'

Did Raffa *have* to turn on the wolfish smile as he leaned one hand against the doorjamb? What toothpaste did he use? He smelled so good he made her hungry, and his teeth were really, really white…

'Did I interrupt something? Only you look…'

Attractively flushed? Horrendously heated? 'No…you didn't interrupt anything.' She drew a confident laugh from her depleted laugh quiver. 'Not at all…I was just hurrying to get everything together.' Fingers crossed behind her back. 'Because I didn't want to hold you up.'

'You didn't… So, did you have time for breakfast?' He brought his arm down and straightened up, so she had that Lilliputian feeling again, compensated by a thrilling glimpse of tanned, stubble-shaded skin above the crisp white business shirt…and the deep blue silk tie…and the dark, sharply tailored suit that was either Armani or Savile Row.

Armani, Casey guessed, instinctively smoothing her chainstore trousers. No. She was wrong. It was Ozwald Boateng. The kingfisher silk lining gave it away. God, he was so sexy. And she was so red-faced—and just everything she had vowed not to be.

'What's that you've got under your arm?' he demanded.

She grimaced. Hair? *Dear God!* Damp patch? *Almost worse.* She had to replay the application of deodorant in her mind before she could relax. 'Oh, you mean my folder?'

'What else?' He frowned attractively. 'May I?'

She handed it over.

'What is this?' He turned it in his hands.

'My preliminary survey of my findings at the shopping mall...'

'You typed it up?' He leafed through the pages.

'I used the business centre at the hotel. My handwriting's dreadful...'

Without even sunglasses to hide his extraordinary eyes, Casey felt as if she were under a particularly penetrating microscope, with her deepest, darkest secrets laid out on a slide while Raffa put his eye to the scope. 'Will I do?' she said, wishing she could cut the nervous laugh; it was making her nervous. She assumed a look of quiet confidence as Raffa's gaze ran swiftly over her.

'You look lovely,' he said.

She did?

No one had ever told her she looked lovely before. She was frequently told she was too intense, too career-orientated, too serious, too driven. And in fairness all of the above was true. Lovely, however, was not a word anyone associated with her.

'Shall we?' he invited, gesturing towards the bank of elevators down the hall.

She had to rip her stare from his face first, which wasn't easy.

So what now? Casey wondered, trying not to make it too obvious that she had to run every now and then to keep up with Raffa. The avenue they were speeding down, which could never be called a corridor in a million years, had a gilded roof that arced above them, decorated with cherubs and rosettes of flowers, while the marble floor was strewn with priceless rugs and guarded by towering pillars garnished with gold leaf, lapis lazuli, and enough light to illuminate small town. So, if this was merely Raffa's flagship hotel, what would his palace be like? Not that she ever expected to see it, of course.

Casey swayed dizzily as they reached the apex of the glass atrium. Was it her fear of heights, her reaction to the sight of Raffa in a business suit looking even sexier than he had in jeans, or the wildest daydream of all—which, if she had been another, bolder person entirely, was to loosen that tie and peel back that jacket?

In front of his bodyguards?

Casey shuddered as the black-clad men emerged from the shadows. She viewed them nervously. Should she greet them or not? She decided *not* when they stared past her.

'You're a woman, and so invisible,' Raffa informed her discreetly.

Oh, good…She had to get used to the idea that Raffa was never alone.

Was Raffa ever alone?

She refused to progress that thought. And as she preceded him into the glass elevator and felt him behind her, like a power source that made all the tiny hairs on the back of her neck stand to attention, she wondered if he somehow sensed her attraction to him and her total ignorance of such things too.

'How do you like the hotel, Casey?'

'A lot—thank you…' She stared fixedly ahead. This wasn't the time to explain that she was terrified of heights, or to acknowledge that they were really high up and travelling down the side of one of the tallest buildings in the city at lightning speed. It was a relief when Raffa moved in front of her, blocking the view— or it might have been if he hadn't been standing quite so close.

'Are you scared of heights?' he said, frowning. 'You should have said. We could have travelled another way.'

Base-jumping, clinging to his back?

She'd put nothing past him.

And now she had nowhere to stare, but at Raffa, and the wide expanse of his chest. The suit he was wearing complemented the depth of his tan, and hinted at enough of the hard form underneath to tease her senses, while the dark blue silk tie picked up the raven's wing highlights in his hair. She could only conclude that his face would always be stubble-shaded, since she had never seen it any other way, and those sensual lips—

'Surely you're not cold?' Raffa observed as she shivered delicately.

'No. I was just thinking.'

'Share your thoughts?'

Her wild, erotic thoughts? Not a chance. She might be gauche and inexperienced, but there was nothing wrong with her imagination. She collected herself with difficulty as the ground rushed up to meet them. 'I was thinking about an article I read in the newspaper.' Out of time sequence, but she was almost telling the truth. 'It mentioned the price paid for a car's licence plate…'

'Tell me more,' he prompted.

'It fetched three million dollars. That's a lot of money. I just wondered if that was the usual result for an auction in A'Qaban?'

Something sparked in his eyes. 'It can be…with the right auctioneer. Why do you ask?'

There was definitely something more; something Raffa wasn't telling her. 'I'm just curious,' Casey admitted. Curious, and wondering how to turn all the cash sloshing around A'Qaban to the good of the country at large. 'Are we heading straight to a meeting?' she asked as the lift slowed, thinking it the perfect opportunity to do some digging.

'We're going to start with a little more getting to know you time first.'

'We are?' Her throat constricted at the thought of Raffa getting to know her better.

'After I introduce you to my team.'

Ah.

'So you can relax now,' he murmured as the glass and steel doors slid open.

How could she do that when he appeared to have perfected the technique of reading her mind?

She slotted in to his team as if she'd been working alongside them for years. They wore Armani, while Casey carried off her pick of chainstore items with effortless grace. She talked the same language, and added some words of her own. This wasn't the ruffled woman who had landed in A'Qaban, but a competent, capable executive, whom anyone could see was more than ready to make the next move up the ladder. She was handling this first meeting with much more aplomb than he had anticipated. Had he been guilty so far of judging Casey on her fragile self-image rather than on her business acumen?

He listened intently as she talked his team through her findings at the mall, and watched with interest as she turned in profile to progress her Power Point presentation. The close-fitting trousers she had chosen in the mall hinted at her figure, while the short, red tailored cardigan clung to her slender shoulders, emphasising the femininity she took such pains to disguise. That puzzled him. What was she frightened of?

By the time he brought the meeting to an end an idea had occurred to him. The successful candidate would be someone who could work as easily outside the office as inside; they must get on confidently with people from all walks of life. And, following on from their earlier conversation, Casey's next test was obvious.

CHAPTER SIX

'WHY are we here?' she said, leaning forward to peer out of the limousine window as they drew up outside one of his warehouses on the dock.

'To show you some things you have to sell.'

'I have to sell them? What? Where?'

'Why don't you wait and see?'

How pretty she was when she did that smile/frown thing. Waving the driver away, he helped her out of the limousine himself. In fact, he was done with drivers.

'Could you have my car delivered?' he asked discreetly, while Casey stood staring up at the outside of the aircraft-hangar-sized warehouse in awe.

'Certainly, sir. Which car would you like?'

Casey's words about excess flew into his mind. She could be his conscience for the day, he decided wryly, asking for the Tesla to be delivered dockside.

'The Tesla? Yes, sir.'

'Come on,' he said, turning to Casey. 'Let's go inside…'

He took her through a small side door into a yawning space, packed with everything from a stretch Hummer to a side room holding enough cutting-edge carbon technology tack for five teams of polo ponies. There was enough excess inside here to give her a blue fit.

'What on earth *is* all this?' she said softly, and he could already hear her mind cogs whirring.

She was probably imagining a store where she would have to put all these things on sale under the same roof, and wondering how on earth she was going to organise it.

'We're not finished yet,' he warned as he led the way down an aisle lined with packing cases stretching high into the silence of the dust-flecked air.

'What *is* all this?' she repeated.

Her voice was tense and excited, though she kept her distance as they walked along.

'You like a challenge, don't you?'

'Yes,' she said cautiously.

'Then let's move on to the inner sanctum.'

There were guards on the door, and a number of pass codes had to be inputted before finally iris recognition allowed him entry. Once they were inside he could see she was surprised by the fact that, compared to the rest of the facility, this was a relatively comfortable and ordinary-looking office. Having shut them inside the hermetically sealed space, he touched a hidden lever, and a safe in the floor began to rise.

'Any more surprises?' she asked him when he glanced at her.

They shared a moment, and this time he let his gaze linger. 'We'll have to see, won't we?' he teased her gently as she looked away. 'I'm not wholly sure what surprises you yet.'

Now she blushed.

Taking a key fob from his pocket, he approached the safe and keyed in the numbers, changed remotely on the fob every few minutes by satellite signal. He heard her gasp when the door sprang open as if by magic. Withdrawing a small leather suitcase, he suggested she sat down.

'I'll bring it over to the table,' he said, 'so you can take a proper look. There are things in here it would be better not to drop…'

* * *

Raffa drew up a chair and sat close by without touching her. It was hard to relax, but she *must* relax if she were to concentrate. She inhaled deeply, drawing on his delicious scent and warmth, allowing her eyes one last greedy glimpse of his strong, pirate's face before putting herself on a strict Raffa-free diet.

She gasped as he showed her the fabulous Fabergé egg. 'Oh, my...' Her voice tailed away.

She had sold many things in her time, but nothing to compare with this. The workmanship was breathtaking in its complexity, and so much more beautiful than any photograph would allow. But she didn't have the know-how required to sell *objets d'art* of this quality, Casey realised, wondering if she was destined to fail this test.

Raffa went on to reveal what amounted to not a king's ransom in jewels, but a Sheikh's. Remembering her bemusement at the price paid for one car registration plate, Casey realised she would have to make some serious adjustments to her thinking. And she would have to stop being distracted by Raffa, who right now was handling the various artefacts with reverence and sensitivity. She had never encountered a man with such power and strength and yet such sensibility. No wonder she was distracted—those hands, that concentration...

She must have quivered involuntarily, for he looked up.

'Are you all right, Casey?' he asked her softly.

She passed a hand across her brow, pretending concentration on a breathtaking collar of emeralds and diamonds which Raffa had just removed from a velvet case. 'So, what kind of retail facility did you have in mind for all this?' she asked him in a voice turned suddenly dry. 'I should own up right away and tell you I have never sold anything of this value before.'

'Very few people have,' he pointed out. 'But you can sell anything, according to your CV.'

'That refers to concepts and schemes rather than fabulous objects like this.'

'Then it's time to stretch yourself,' Raffa countered.

How had their heads become so close their faces were almost touching? They were both leaning over the glittering mound of jewels on the table like two children examining a pirate's hoard; both of them with eyes bright with the light of possibility. Though Casey guessed hers was the only heart trying to beat its way out of a chest.

'So, what do you think?' Raffa said as he toyed with the magnificent emerald and diamond necklace.

Everything she shouldn't, Casey thought, wishing she could concentrate on the only thing that mattered—which was the job she was here to try out for.

'Casey?' Raffa prompted.

She snapped her brain onto full alert. 'I think I should hire experts to advise and assist me,' she said. 'But I *will* sell these for you.'

'Good,' he said, settling back. 'Though I think sapphires would suit you better,' he added, as Casey distractedly toyed with the emerald necklace.

'You do?' She made the very serious mistake of looking at him questioningly.

'Yes, I do,' he murmured.

She swallowed deep as, having selected a fabulous sapphire necklace from the hoard in front of them, Raffa used one hand to brush her long hair to one side before looping the glinting band of royal blue stones around her neck. She was suddenly acutely conscious of the silence between them, and of her own unsteady breathing. She couldn't move or break the spell, and though she was wearing her hair neatly tied in a ribbon, and was in every way modestly dressed, her prim exterior bore no relation to the hot thoughts racing through her head.

It was another forceful reminder that having no experience of sex was no guarantee that she would never think about it. Vividly. And, yes, at the most inopportune of moments. Like now...when the warm touch of Raffa's fingers on her collar-bone was making it so hard to remain still, and when the heavy platinum collar he was placing round her neck felt like a restraining device of a wickedly erotic kind—one that should horrify her, but instead tempted her to sigh and roll her head as the cool metal met her skin.

As if this wasn't dangerous enough, when Raffa snapped the catch into place her body yearned for him. 'I'd better not get used to this,' she said out loud. Coming determinedly to her senses, she reached up, removed the necklace and handed it back to him.

'It doesn't hurt to indulge in a little fantasy shopping once in a while.'

'As long as you don't confuse fantasy with reality,' Casey agreed. As she watched Raffa replace the priceless jewels in their nest, Casey murmured, 'I wonder who they are destined for?'

Raffa's sharp glance caught her out. For all her brave words about fantasy and reality, she had never been short of imagination.

'You never know, I might want to keep them,' she said, laughing to make light of it.

'Then I'd better lock them away…'

His gaze held hers for a moment. Was it possible to want a man so badly? Or to be so frightened of the consequences of those feelings?

Raffa appeared not to notice these darker thoughts as he replaced the jewels in their velvet case. 'Sapphires suit you,' he said. 'You should remember that. They're the same colour as your eyes…'

'Oh, I will,' Casey assured him with a wry smile. 'Next time I go jewellery-shopping I'll put sapphires at the top of my list.' She was deadpan. They really did inhabit different worlds.

Raffa smiled too. His was more of an eyes glinting, tongue in cheek kind of smile. So he *did* have a sense of humour. 'Do you have jewels in every colour?' she asked in a posh voice, acting the customer and trying not to giggle.

It backfired on her. Raffa took hold of her hands in a firm

grasp. She gulped as she stared at his strong hands resting over hers and felt a terrible yearning inside her.

'Hold your hands like this…' He formed her hands into a supplicant's bowl. 'Ready?'

She nodded stiffly as he steadied his amused gaze on her. 'Ready,' she whispered hoarsely.

Picking up a drawstring bag, he loosened the cord and tipped a heap of polished gemstones into her hands. There was every colour imaginable.

'And these are what I've got to sell? I really am going to need some help.' She was already frowning as she thought about where to find the appropriate experts.

'If you can't do it—'

'I *can* do it.' She met Raffa's gaze and saw that it had changed. There was no warmth now; just rigorous expectation. 'I'll find who I need to help me with current market valuations. I'll be fine,' she said firmly. 'My only concern is that wherever I have to sell these there must be a secure environment in which to display them and for my staff to work.'

'You can leave that to me,' Raffa told her. 'Anything else?'

'Other than that, I see my only problem being moving stock quickly enough to satisfy your demands and—'

'Wrong,' Raffa interrupted. 'I don't expect you to sell them.'

Casey frowned, waiting for an explanation, hoping it wouldn't be too long coming, so she didn't have to keep on staring at Raffa's fiercely handsome face. 'Can you explain?'

'You're going to auction them,' he said.

Casey sat back, stunned, her head swimming with insecurity. She was a businesswoman, yes, but she was a backroom girl, not an extrovert. She stood no chance of whipping up a sophisticated crowd into a buying frenzy.

'Your task is to do this at a charity event that means a lot to me,' Raffa explained.

'And the event is…?'

'A grand ball in three days' time to honour my…' His lips tugged.

'Your recent coronation?' Casey suggested.

Raffa's lips pressed down wryly. 'You can call it what you want. The main thing is that the charity benefits on the night.'

But for all his dismissive talk she saw his gaze grow serious; there was a vision for his country in his eyes.

'The money will go to help my Bedouin communities.'

'Please tell me about them,' she said, as he hit on the one topic that enthused her most of all.

'They are a travelling people, and we provide them with flying ambulances, travelling teachers, medical facilities…'

Not surprisingly, she was instantly sold on the idea of raising money for this worthy cause at the auction, and as Raffa continued to explain she knew he wasn't a king in name only, but a leader—a man who was modest in the midst of excess, a man whose first thought would always be for his people.

'This auction…' Casey's mouth dried when she thought about the responsibility Raffa had given her. He couldn't know how terrified she would be, standing up in front of the sort of people who would be attending such a royal event. But if this was a test she must approach it like any other, and she had the most worthy cause to fight for; that should give her courage. 'I won't let you down,' she said.

'Don't let our Bedouin down,' he said. 'We'll all be relying on you to raise as much money as you can.'

She grew serious as she thought about it. 'There's a lot of product here, as well as in the warehouse. How long do I have?' She grimaced, thinking about the logistics of moving so many items off the shelf.

'If you're in any doubt, you should pull out now.'

The incredible sums of money involved did worry her—if only because she had never been involved in anything like this before. But, remembering the fabulous amount paid for that licence plate, she knew there were riches in A'Qaban. She also knew people became donation-exhausted after a while, however wealthy they were. She would have to be innovative if the fund was to reach its potential.

'What are you thinking?' Raffa prompted.

'That I can't hold this auction the usual way.'

'How many ways are there to conduct an auction?'

Before she could answer he moved his chair back—impatiently, she thought. He snapped the catches on the suitcase containing the jewels, he locked it again before returning it to the safe. And then, as she might have predicted, instead of coming to sit down, he started to prowl up and down the small room.

She was on a knife edge, Casey realised. She must convince Raffa she could do this. He might have thrown her a curve ball, that she had no intention of dropping it.

She stood too. Unfortunately, even drawn to her full height she barely reached Raffa's shoulder. He stood watching her with his eyes narrowed and keen, like a sleek black panther with a thorn in its paw. The thought of soothing him by touching his arm was a giant step too far, and so instead she stood stiffly to attention. 'You can rely on me absolutely. I promise I'll do this for you.'

'You're quite sure?'

'Positive.'

An electric current snapped between them. It held them together and held them apart. But if she was going to work with the most dangerously handsome man on the planet she would have to get used to a few fireworks going off inside her, Casey reasoned. She'd just have to use them to fire her determination. 'I'll have help to organise the event, I take it?' She was already off and running. Her mind had jumped three days ahead and was rapidly filling in the blank spaces in between.

'You'll have professional party-planners and my team. All you have to do is handle the auction. If I can give you a word of advice—use your strengths.'

'I intend to.'

'Good. Sell the goods and get the most you can for them. That's it.'

That's it? Raffa's gesture had encompassed not just this small room, but the warehouse outside. He really did have a different set of perspectives.

'Thank you for entrusting me with such an important task.'

He didn't like that. His brow rose. 'I employ the best, Casey. I expect the best from them. Nothing less will do. If you fail—'

It was like being on a see-saw—first up, then down; she had better make sure her next move wasn't out, Casey concluded. 'I won't fail.'

They stared at each other like combatants across a ring, each of them measuring the other.

'Whatever happens, unsold items can be offered on the open market after the auction,' Raffa explained. 'But you'll make more during the auction, so I'm relying on you to appeal to each individual's…'

'Better nature?' Casey suggested.

'Exactly,' Raffa agreed, sharing an ironic look with her.

'Then please leave it to me,' she said, feeling quietly confident suddenly, as right out of the blue an idea occurred to her.

Casey stared in surprise at the low-slung roadster waiting for them by the kerb. 'No Lamborghini?' She turned to Raffa.

'No limousine either…' His lips curved, making her heart bounce. 'Knowing your distaste of excess, I thought I'd introduce you to my new green baby.'

'Green?' Casey's forehead pleated with disbelief as she stared at the speed monster crouched on the road.

'This is the latest in electric vehicles,' Raffa explained, walking round the impressive sports car. 'She does nought to sixty in three point nine seconds, making her somewhat faster than a Lotus and almost on a par with my Ferrari, and yet she costs me less than one penny per mile to run.'

'She?' She should have known better, Casey realized, as

Raffa ran one hand lovingly across the flanks of his new motor car. 'And it's cheap to buy, of course?' she said, tongue in cheek.

Raffa shot a glance at her that made her cheeks fire up.

'It's very…striking,' she admitted, back-pedalling rapidly. In fact, the sleek black beast was the perfect servant of its master.

'Go on,' Raffa prompted her dryly. 'Say it, Casey.'

'Say what?' She tensed.

'It's sexy…'

Yes, it was—and so was he. But no way was she getting into that.

He had decided to take Casey somewhere she could relax, and where they could continue getting the measure of each other. If she was going to be working for him he had to get to know her, and if she pulled off this auction she would be a real contender for the job. She didn't know it yet, but all the other applicants had backed out by this stage, or he'd sent them home. If one of the others had offered to run his auction he would have thought it bravado, and wouldn't have trusted them to do it, but something about Casey suggested he should give her a chance. He'd have someone ready and waiting in the wings in case she got stage fright. This charity was too important to risk on his whim. But as whims went…

'Get in,' he said, when she hesitated by the car door.

'Where are we going?'

She was so wary. It gave him a jolt to see how quickly she could change from confident businesswoman to this. 'I'm going to take you for a well-earned drink,' he said. 'Maybe lunch, if you'd like? Well? What are you waiting for? It isn't rocket science; yes or no?'

She was waiting for courage and self-belief. She was wondering how to handle all the personal insecurities she felt as a woman, with this man who had no insecurities at all, and how to handle feelings for him that had no connection with the job.

* * *

Raffa took her to what had to be the most fashionable club in the city, judging by the fabulous array of gleaming vehicles parked outside. It wasn't as if they wouldn't be noticed here, she thought, but Raffa didn't seem to care. He made no attempt to claim special status as the manager of the club hurried to greet them.

'Are you ready?' he said, offering her his arm.

She'd bet the glamorous women entering the club in front of them with their handsome escorts hadn't picked out *their* clothes from the bargain rail. It seemed incredible that she was about to take the arm of the ruling Sheikh. But as she did she realised his bodyguards were just an invisible step away. 'Do they have to come with us?' she asked. She found them so intrusive and forbidding.

'They don't have to do anything you don't want them to…'

She felt his strength then, and just for a moment experienced what it would be like to have a man like Raffa in her life. She felt cherished and protected when she was with him.

But she wasn't *with* Raffa, Casey reminded herself before her imagination ran away with her. He was her boss and he was taking her to lunch. And the touch of his hand on her arm…and his body brushing against hers…

'Why are you shivering? Are you cold?' he said as the *maître d'* led them inside.

Cold? Did frigid translate into A'Qabani?

Raffa gave her a reassuring squeeze. 'Courage,' he murmured, his warm breath brushing her ear. 'Many of your potential buyers at the auction will be here. You do want to give them the right impression, don't you?'

Of course she did. And those few words tipped the balance of the internal see-saw inside her back to business.

As she glanced around the exclusive club Casey realised that some of the younger women present appeared to be glued to every word their companions had to say. They laughed on cue, stared in awe on cue, and rarely spoke unless they were asked a direct question. How long was she going to last here?

It would be useful research, her business head reminded her.

'Could we sit somewhere where I can people-watch?'

'If you'd find it helpful…' he replied. 'Champagne?' Raffa suggested once they were settled at a table.

'I'd prefer juice?'

'Juice it is.'

This was new for him—this woman who could be one thing in the boardroom and a shy fawn-like creature in her private life. He supposed it was his reward for mixing business with pleasure; something he'd never done before.

But this interview process must never become something more. Casey's innocence prevented it. She was so tender and vulnerable outside her job, and that should never be exploited. And besides, with so much appetite on his side and so much untapped passion on hers, if their relationship ever did overstep the mark they would take off into sexual space and never come back to earth again.

As he watched her moist lips embrace the straw plunged deep into fresh papaya juice, he could only be thankful she hadn't agreed to champagne. He needed a clear head and all his sternest resolve if this apparently innocent meeting in a club was going to remain the safe side of sin.

CHAPTER SEVEN

'TELL me something about your family, Casey…'

'My family?' Casey's throat constricted as Raffa leaned towards her. Was her family being considered for the job now? She made herself calm down by reasoning that this was a perfectly acceptable question for an employer to ask. It was by no means unique, and it allowed Raffa to paint a clearer picture of who she was. But still…

'We're nothing special.'

'Nothing special?' Raffa frowned, his dark eyes glinting in the discreet lighting. 'Why don't you let me be the judge of that?'

'I'm sure you'd find us terribly boring.'

'And I'm equally sure I won't…' As he spoke Raffa straightened up and put his hands flat on the table, where the delicious entrées they had ordered lay largely untouched.

They had a lot to say to each other, Casey reflected, except when it came to their private lives; then both of them clammed up. But she didn't have the option of holding out on him if she wanted this job. 'You've read my file—'

'So I know a lot about you on paper,' he countered. 'But I want you to *tell* me. My intention in bringing you here to A'Qaban is to go way beyond the printed page, Casey. I need to know you.'

'I understand…'

'And I understand that your parents' job is a little unusual,' he said in a reassuring voice. 'So don't feel embarrassed.'

'I'm not...' His hard mouth had softened fractionally, she noticed, and there was genuine warmth in his eyes.

'Why don't you tell me about them?'

'I'm okay with their work,' she admitted, hearing in her voice that she had made it sound like a lie.

'Expand a little,' Raffa encouraged, pouring a glass of water for her.

How much did he want to know? She had never discussed her parents' work with anyone outside the family before. How could she, when she could never take a man home to 'meet the family', knowing that any boyfriend would only end up as a lab rat to be quizzed and evaluated by her sex therapist parents before being added to their latest batch of trial statistics.

'Do you know my parents' work?'

'I know their work well,' he said, as casually as if her parents ran a market garden. 'They're world-renowned academics; it would be hard not to.'

He wasn't mocking her, as so many others had. He was genuinely interested, she realised.

'I never forget we are all products of our background, to some extent, and so it's only natural for me to be curious about your formative influences.'

'And about whether I can talk of them without embarrassment?' she said bluntly. 'I'm proud of my parents' achievements.' She was. They had helped so many people. Except for her, of course. But it went without saying that *that* had never been on the cards.

'So you've grown up in a loving family?'

'Absolutely. My parents may seem unconventional to some people, but they always put me first and were very good role models.'

Raffa eased back, appearing to consider this. She was overheating. It was the first time she had talked so openly about a side of her life that, for all the sex talk round the dinner table, was repressed. In spite of the casual way her parents discussed intimacy, she had never found it possible to open up. Her parents had heard it all before, she had reasoned when she was younger, and she knew it would only embarrass them to realise what a failure their daughter was in an area in which they specialised.

'You're very lucky,' Raffa said. 'Tragically, I never knew my parents.'

His manner prevented further discussion, and she respected his silence. What she had so reluctantly revealed was insignificant by comparison to what Raffa had just told her. It was so totally unexpected she sat stunned for a moment. They had both opened up—perhaps more than they had intended to. How often did that happen? Casey wondered.

'That's why this country means so much to me.' Raffa's eyes were burning with passion. 'I am investing everything I have, everything I am, in the future of A'Qaban. I have trained my whole life for this moment.'

Raffa's words moved her deeply and her own concerns paled into insignificance. But he didn't need her to be 'moved', he needed action—and she was confident she could give him exactly what he wanted if he would give her the chance.

'I'll support you in any way I can,' she assured him. 'We're going to make a success of this.'

Raffa stood up, preparing to leave. 'Why do I believe you, Casey Michaels?'

'Because I haven't let you down yet?' The wry tug of her lips acknowledged that she hadn't been tested yet either. But she *would* come through for him. She savoured the moment her hand remained in Raffa's warm, secure grip. She would run this auction for him and his charity and make it work—whatever it took.

Releasing her hand, Raffa shot a look at his no-nonsense steel watch. This was the signal that brought their informal lunch meeting to a close. There was a subtle change in him, she thought, as if he had returned everything to a strictly business footing. Which it always had been for him, she reminded herself.

They left the club with Raffa's security guards falling into silent formation behind them. Some people outside on the pavement braved the guards' stern, forbidding faces to call out in support of their new young leader. As Raffa paused to acknowledge these salutations Casey thought how fine the line was between success and disaster. She had so very nearly been sent home on the next plane, and now she had been given a task that exceeded even her wildest expectations.

'Am I walking too fast for you?' Raffa turned to look for her.

'No, this is just fine,' she said, hurrying after him. Tilting her chin at a determined angle, she assured him, 'Don't you worry, I'll keep up…'

Casey shivered with awareness as Raffa held the car door for her. She passed close enough to feel his energy and inhale his cologne. Her parents had told her that it would take a certain type of man to end Casey's self-imposed chastity. And she had no doubt Raffa was that type of man. But imagining anything would happen between them was shooting for the stars, and she was certain that this wasn't what her serious-minded parents had had in mind for her.

'I have a question for you,' he said as they settled in the car.

She had to shake her mind free of the illusory promise of erotic instruction at his hands and focus carefully. He would be a master of the art. Raffa had that sort of promise in his eyes. *Shake it off!*

'Yes?'

'If you had to live in A'Qaban, Casey, could you?'

She gave him her honest thoughts. 'I'd have to—at least until I was confident my side of the operation over here was running smoothly.'

'But could you?' he repeated.

She resisted the lure of Raffa's firm, sensual lips, only to lock in combat with his stare. 'I'll live anywhere I must in order to give the most to my job.'

'Wouldn't your parents miss you?'

'Of course they would, and I'd miss them dreadfully—but, as they quote Kahlil Gibran to me non-stop, I'm guessing they'd be a little bit pleased for me too.'

'Khalil Gibran? The Lebanese-American author and philosopher?' His dark eyes lit with remembered pleasure. 'Do you remember the quote?'

'Of course I do.' She smiled. '"You are the bows from which your children as living arrows are sent forth."'

There was a moment of stillness and then Raffa nodded his head, reminding Casey that he'd been forced by tragedy to be both bow and arrow.

As he started the engine she noticed the scar on his face for the first time. It ran from just below his eye to the corner of his mouth, and must have been the result of a serious injury. She guessed it was a legacy of his time in the Special Forces, and wondered how hard that had been for Raffa, with no family to anchor him. He had hinted at some catastrophe in his youth, and she guessed it must have denied him the love she'd known.

She was gaining in confidence all the time, Casey realised, and a lot of that was due to Raffa. It was time to remind herself that he was a king, and that she was growing far too interested in him.

Too interested? She could so very easily fall in love with a man with whom she seemed to share many of the same goals, Casey realised with a jolt, as Raffa released the brake and turned the wheel in the direction of her hotel.

Having furnished her with an inventory of the items she would have to sell, Raffa left Casey at the door to her suite.

'And I have how long to do this?' she said, fingering the thick sheaf of paper.

'Forty-eight hours.'

'Forty-eight—' She almost choked, but remembered it was crucial to remain positive and clear-headed if she was to have a chance of doing this. 'Forty-eight hours,' she repeated. Her thoughts might be tumbling over each other in disarray, but there could be no excuses.

'Sorry—duty calls,' Raffa said, fielding a call on his phone. Duty would always call Raffa. She knew that.

'I'm sorry to rush away,' he said, touching her arm lightly and leaving an electric charge in his wake. 'We'll finish this later.'

'No problem. Goodbye—' But Raffa was already on his way.

Wanting to put the idea that had occurred to her earlier into a more formal structure, Casey decided to burn the midnight oil. Late that night, having taken a shower, she changed into pyjamas and called for pizza and coffee. While she was waiting for the food to arrive, she started making notes. She knew exactly how she was going to handle the auction. The plan she'd come up with would do exactly as Raffa had suggested and make the most of her strengths…

She was on her second cup of coffee when the doorbell rang. She remained where she was, hoping the invisible butler was still on duty, but the bell rang again. She reached distractedly for the intercom, her mind still half on her plan.

'Raffa?' Casey blenched. Raffa was not just in the building, he was at the door.

The space between the desk and the bathroom had never felt so far, but she had to grab a robe. Belting it tightly, she slipped her feet into slippers and with her heart thundering ten to the dozen ran back again to let him in.

How magnificent he looked in a tailored suit. Even with the earring and disreputable-looking stubble he was an imposing sight. And so was the team of businessmen and women standing in formation behind him.

Swinging the door shut with a gasp, she pulled it open just enough for him to hear her whisper, 'Did you need something?'

'May we come in?'

That was not a request, Casey gathered. 'Could you give me a minute?'

'Two minutes?' Raffa suggested dryly.

She closed the door with barely a click. Two minutes to call room service, find clothes more suitable for a business meeting than her teddy bear print pyjamas, and summon the invisible butler from wherever he hung out. Shouldering the phone, she ordered juice, coffee, iced water and pastries. Scraping her hair back on her way to the bathroom, she secured it in the band she always wore round her wrist. Scrubbing her teeth, she gargled with mouthwash before tearing into the bedroom, where she tugged on her work clothes and forced a pair of shoes onto her feet more or less simultaneously.

'Please come in,' she invited two minutes later, hitting the deadline square on the nail.

He leafed through the notes Casey had prepared for him. Her handwriting *was* bad, but she had bullet-pointed everything, and her ideas leapt off the page. They were great.

'This is good,' he said briefly, before handing it around.

Casey's ideas were unique and fresh, and he was glad he had passed responsibility for running the auction over to her. His only problem was with the large reception room they were using for this meeting. It was the same place he'd seen her half naked, and it was proving to be a real distraction. His position was clear, he reminded himself sternly. Casey was pure. He was not. She was under his protection.

Which wasn't nearly enough to stop him wanting her.

The muted murmurs of Raffa's team discussing her proposal provided a soothing soundtrack to Casey's turbulent thoughts. Raffa watched his board members while she watched him. He glanced up once, and, seeing her looking at him, turned away. She knew her cheeks must be flushed, betraying her, but something made her look at him again…and this time their gazes held. Was Raffa approving her or warning her?

Thankfully, her body quivered a warning, which was enough to make her excuse herself from the table. At precisely that moment the invisible butler chose to make a welcome appearance at the head of a team of waiters with their midnight feast.

'Thank you—just put it down over here, would you, please?' Casey murmured as the discussion of her proposals continued to gather momentum around the table. She'd return in a minute and add her own thoughts to the discussion, but in the meantime…Was she imagining Raffa's gaze on her back? She tensed, every sense on high alert. She concentrated hard on showing the waiters where to put things. 'Thank you,' she said to them again, handing over the tip she'd kept by.

'You've thought of everything,' Raffa murmured, appearing by her side.

'Coffee?' she said, struggling for normality in a world full of just one man.

'Coffee would be good for everyone at this point.'

Raffa called a ten-minute break while she tried to ignore the effect his deep rich baritone was having on her senses.

'No one wants to stop talking,' he said, returning to her side. 'They're too enthused by your plan.'

'I'm pleased they like it.'

'Like it? They own it already.'

'It's only in the planning stages at the moment,' she pointed out. 'But if you think it's what you want…'

'It is what I want.'

His gaze strayed to her lips. She tried hard not to react or show by any means that her body yearned to be touched by him.

'Shall we return to the table?' Raffa suggested, as if this highly charged moment had never happened.

She practically galloped there.

They finally broke at three in the morning, by which time Casey was wide awake. But, as Raffa pointed out, they all ought to get some sleep as they had to start again first thing in the morning. *This* morning, Casey reflected as the team filed out. It was hardly worth going to bed.

Raffa was the last to leave. During the course of the meeting he had taken off his suit jacket and loosened his tie, and his shirt was unbuttoned at the neck, revealing a tempting few inches of hard, bronzed flesh. With his sleeves rolled back, revealing hard muscled forearms, he was quite a distraction—one she hadn't had the chance to appreciate fully during the meeting. As she said goodbye to him he looked at her another beat too long. His stubble was blacker than ever, making him look like a buccaneer. He made her feel very small and not very safe, and suddenly she wasn't sure what to say next. A brisk goodnight was safest, Casey concluded, reaching for the door handle.

She drew a swift intake of breath when Raffa's hand covered hers. *Was this the moment?* She remained motionless as he lightly ran the knuckles of one hand down her cheek.

'You did well tonight, Casey...'

'Thank you...' Everything slipped out of focus while she examined the effect Raffa had on her inexperienced body.

That had to be why it took her a moment to realise he'd gone.

CHAPTER EIGHT

CASEY let her clothes lie where they fell and collapsed into bed. She'd probably been unconscious before her head had hit the pillow, she realised when the bedside alarm rang. She hadn't noticed how tired she was—but Raffa had. Was that why he had left her so abruptly? She traced the path his hand had taken down her face. She still wore the memory of his touch, which led seamlessly on to wondering how the rest of her might feel now if he had continued his explorations.

Don't even think that way, she told herself firmly, swinging her legs over the side of the divan. She was innocent, she was inexperienced, and this was business. She might have had only three hours' sleep, but another working day had started and she had to be ready for anything Raffa threw at her.

The phone was ringing when she came out of the bathroom. She pounced on it, thrilling at the sound of the familiar voice—though she started smiling when she heard his words. 'This time don't tell me you're ready if you're not.'

'Give me five minutes.'

'I'm in the lobby.'

And pacing up and down, Casey guessed as the line went dead.

Raffa took Casey to the venue where the auction would be held. It was the ballroom of his latest hotel. He showed her the guest list, as well as the table plan she'd asked to see. She said it was crucial to understand the rivalries between the various tables, and that was where he could help out. By lunchtime she had a good overview, and had convinced Raffa that he had a strong new team member in Casey Michaels. He had only one small niggle left. Casey could pull people together and work effectively in a team, but could she whip jaded billionaires into a frenzy of competition? That remained to be seen. Meanwhile…

'Lunch?' he suggested.

'I've no time for lunch,' she said as a florist arrived.

'Delegate,' he said, taking hold of her arm.

'But, Raffa, I—'

'Can you delegate or not? You're no good to me if you can't.'

'I can delegate.'

'Then do so. Give the florist credit for knowing what she's doing. You can't handle everything single-handedly, Casey.' His eyes lit with humour. 'Even *I* can't do that.'

He took her to his private elevator. Discreet and luxurious, it played host to one man. There were no bodyguards here, and no glass walls. There was just one man and one woman on a three-hundred-metre trip to a fabulous penthouse that took up the whole of the top floor.

He brought the elevator to a halt halfway to its destination. Casey stared at him in alarm. 'Is something wrong?' she asked.

'Absolutely.' As he spoke he placed one fist against the wall next to her face, effectively pinning her in position.

She stared at him. Her eyes darkened. 'I don't understand…'

'I think you do.'

'Did you lean on the controls by accident?'

'Have some confidence in yourself, Casey.'

She looked at him, and then her glance flickered away.

'Would you *like* me to say I leaned on the controls by accident? Would that make you feel more relaxed?' He angled his head to look at her—to drink her in. She was aroused, and their lips were only inches apart. 'Yes?' he prompted when she remained silent. She eased her shoulders in a tiny shrug and looked away, but he cupped her chin and made her look at him. 'Believe in yourself, Casey…'

Her breathing was unsteady in the silence, and he remembered how innocent she was. The comfortable banquette, the mirror and accommodating padded wall would all have to go to waste, he accepted.

'Are you hungry?' he murmured.

'I'm starving,' she said with relief.

'Then I'm going to feed you.' As he spoke he activated the control that would take the elevator the rest of the way up. 'I'm afraid it will only be a lunchtime snack,' he warned, 'since we don't have time for the type of banquet I have in mind.'

Her eyes widened. She was off in her fantasy world, he realised. Her lips were swollen with arousal, as if he had kissed them for hours, and her blue eyes had turned black with just the tiniest rim of sapphire remaining. He turned away to give her a moment, ruffling his hair as he stared into the mirror.

'Do you like sushi?' he said then.

'I love sushi.'

'Sushi it is, then,' he said, smiling at her infectious enthusiasm.

In Casey's opinion everyone deserved at least one fairytale in their life. And this was hers, she thought as Raffa led her over the threshold of his fabulous apartment. She wasn't a fairy princess, but a rather ordinary girl from the north of England who happened to have a talent for marketing—but look where that talent had brought her! She was standing at the side of the hottest man in town, in the middle of an interior designer's dream.

'What do you think?' Raffa said, turning to her.

With the light flooding in from the floor-to-ceiling windows overlooking the harbour, she thought that he looked magnificent…that he looked like a true warrior king of the desert, with his powerful legs firmly planted in his golden lion kingdom…

Was everything made of gold?

'Vulgar, isn't it?' he said.

She blinked, trying to take in the apartment and give him her honest opinion—but he was so distracting. 'I think it's lovely, actually,' she admitted. What was a fairytale if it was all magnolia walls and plain furniture? This was luxury such as she had never seen before, luxury on an unprecedented scale, and she thought it absolutely perfect for her lion of the desert.

'Just try to bear in mind this is a hotel room and not my home,' Raffa told her dryly.

A hotel room? Right. They really did come from two different worlds. Hotel rooms in Casey's world came with a bed, a chair and a Formica desk.

'Describe what you see in one sentence,' Raffa suggested.

'Fabulousness pumped up on gold dust and dressed like a movie set fit for a king?'

'Bravo!' He laughed, strong even teeth a flash of brilliant white against his bronzed face.

With her heart thundering like an express train she took a look around to distract herself…Venetian glass, Italian leather, and a vast wall of windows overlooking the marina and the turquoise ocean far below. On the walls Fauvist paintings, flaunting colour. She crossed the room to take a closer look at them, remembering Fauvist was French for wild beast. Casey smiled. Someone here really had a sense of humour.

'Do you like them?' Raffa asked as she went to take a closer look at a Matisse.

'I love them. They're so vibrant…' And she was trembling all over. Her enthusiasm could so easily get the better of her, Casey realised, reining it in. She was alone with Raffa in his apartment; this was not the time to get carried away.

'I'm glad you like them. Which one is your favourite?'

The group of naked people, dancing free, hand in hand around a grassy mound…

'The townscape…'

'Ah, the view of Collioure…'

'Yes, that's the one,' she lied.

Raffa's darkly luminous stare had followed her gaze, and now he looked openly disbelieving. She had told a silly lie that only betrayed her lack of sexual confidence. Lucky for her that wasn't a consideration for him when it came to deciding on the best candidate for the job.

Seated on facing sofas a safe distance apart, they settled down to enjoy the food the waiters brought them. The tempting platters of savoury and sweet delicacies were delicious, as was the freshly squeezed mango juice served with ice and fizzy water.

And Raffa was delicious too. Everything about him said he was a sensualist, a man of potent sexuality who would be completely without inhibition in the bedroom. Maybe he could help her…Maybe she should find out…

Maybe she should pull herself together, Casey's sensible self advised.

'I'm going to suggest something to you,' Raffa said, breaking the spell. 'And I'll be angry if you refuse me.'

Casey's mouth turned dry. She found it wasn't quite that easy to pull herself together—especially when Raffa got up from the sofa and proceeded to come round the table towards her.

'I know how difficult you can be about money…'

With her bubble well and truly burst, she frowned. 'I'm not difficult.'

'Stubborn, then?' he suggested, clearing his throat to hide his laugh.

'Absolutely not.' She was as stubborn as a mule, but with one eye on the job she wasn't about to admit to it.

'Well, if you're so compliant and easygoing, why don't you sit down and relax while I tell you what I've got in mind?'

It took her a moment to realise the most dangerous thing in Raffa's hand was his wallet. 'You carry money?'

'Of course I do. What century do you think this is?'

'And what's *that* for?' She stared suspiciously at the credit card he was holding out to her.

'Do you have a gown for the ball, Cinderella?'

'Cinderella?' Casey's eyes narrowed.

Raffa clearly enjoyed baiting her. Holding up his hands in mock surrender, he said, 'Let me put this another way. You surely don't think I'm such a lousy employer I expect you to pay for the ballgown you'll be forced to wear at the auction? Think of it as a uniform,' he said, tongue in cheek. 'It might sit better with your conscience that way. Unless, of course…' here he paused, eyes glowing with humour '…you have a little something tucked away in your backpack I don't know about?'

'Like a catwalk creation?' As she looked at him her lips threatened rebellion too.

'Just so long as you don't turn up in jeans and flip-flops.'

'Or a safari suit?' she suggested.

They held each other's gaze like old friends who were accustomed to teasing each other.

'You can show this anywhere,' Raffa explained, holding out his gold card, 'and buy anything you want. It will all be charged to my account, no questions asked.'

'Except by me.' It was Casey's turn to bring the conversation to a halt. 'I'm sure I can find something—'

'Appropriate?' Raffa cut across her. 'I'm sure you can too. But I want you to have something special—something that makes you feel like a queen.'

'And I need to wear something expensive for that?'

'What you spend is up to you. I just want you to feel good.'

Any more argument and she'd sound churlish, Casey thought, staring at the plastic Raffa was holding out to her. 'Thank you…' She took the card and put it safely away.

'Don't stint yourself. Shoes, make-up, jewellery—whatever you need, buy.'

His driver arrived, and Raffa explained that he would take

Casey wherever she wanted to go. 'I think you're going to have fun,' he said.

And Raffa sounded as if he meant every word. It made her doubly determined to land the job and repay every penny.

CHAPTER NINE

CASEY thought she had prepared well enough for her entry into the ballroom, but she was wrong. It was full of the most sophisticated people she had ever seen, all dancing to the strains of a full orchestra, and everyone without exception was in evening dress. Some of the men wore orders over one shoulder, and medals, while the women were in a rainbow-hued selection of couture gowns.

Taking a really deep breath, she tried hanging on to the moment the personal shopper had exclaimed with genuine relief after a whole raft of failures, 'This is the one!'

She hoped Raffa would approve of the gown. She had tried to strike a balance between modest and fashionable. Anything else in her favour was down to the team of women who had worked on her all day today, endlessly primping and plucking and polishing and buffing. This was their moment, Casey thought, preparing to walk down the steep flight of stairs.

Like every other man with blood running through their veins, he stopped midway through a conversation to stare at Casey, who was standing framed beneath an archway of flowers at the top of the stairs.

She had taken his advice and spoiled herself for once...

Taken his advice? She had gone so far beyond his advice he was transfixed. The diamonds must have come from Harry

Winston, and the gown she was wearing—flesh-coloured and form-fitting—defied description. Except to say that it was fabulous.

And so was she.

The gown, in floating silk chiffon, criss-crossed Casey's breasts before falling in an elegant column to the floor, making her look like a Greek goddess. It exposed her peach-tinted shoulders, but in deference to the traditionalists amongst them she had covered herself with a wisp of beaded silk. Her hair was dressed up, in a way that suited her, with a few tendrils loose around her face, and she hardly needed the fresh flower in the soft blonde chignon to ornament the outfit when she was already the most fragrant woman in the room.

A woman, he noticed now, who had chosen to wear the most ridiculously high-heeled sandals he'd ever seen—which meant he had to get up there before there was an accident. Making his excuses to the ambassador, he headed straight for the loveliest woman in the room.

The most promising candidate, he corrected himself sternly as he strode quickly up the stairs.

The sight of Raffa sweeping up the stairs in regal robes held her spellbound. She should have known the ruler of A'Qaban would be wearing robes of state for such an important event. She should have known that if Raffa had looked good in Savile Row, and even better in jeans, he would look totally fabulous in flowing Arabian robes of night-blue silk.

'May I escort you?' he said, offering his arm. 'Take it,' he insisted firmly, 'before you land in a heap at the feet of the people you're expecting to cajole and charm tonight.'

'Yes, Your Majesty…' Aware that the eyes of the room were upon them, she dropped a low curtsey, and as she did so she registered a huge erotic charge. Playing dress-up with a king was far more exciting than any fantasy she'd ever managed to come up with.

* * *

He was pleased to see how greatly Casey had grown in confidence, but a little less pleased to realise they were both intensely aware of each other, even in a room full of people. He knew she could feel his interest, and he liked the fact that Casey's gaze was no longer uncertain, but direct, intelligent, and challenging enough to hold his interest. Added to which, she walked like a queen at his side, and he found her company a source of constant stimulation as he introduced her round. But none of that was good for business—or for his vaunted self-control.

The rustle of Raffa's heavy blue silk robes made her think of the hard-muscled form underneath. As he moved around the ballroom introducing her to people it was a struggle not to be distracted—something every other woman present was having trouble with too, Casey noticed. Who could blame them when Raffa's charm was edged with hard and rugged splendour? His robes were trimmed with gold, like the *agal* on his headdress, and there was a dangerous looking dagger at his waist. And a tassel at his neck…

She leaned a little closer, inhaling as she realised the tassel was scented.

'Do you like the aroma of vanilla and sandalwood?' he murmured.

She blushed and pulled away, realising she had invaded the ruler of A'Qaban's personal space to an unforgivable degree. 'I like it very much…' Was it possible *not* to like the scent of warm, clean, sexy man?

'You're right in thinking the tassel is scented,' he explained. 'It's part of my traditional dress, like the *khanjar* at my waist— my dagger,' he prompted.

'Your dagger?' Casey repeated, feeling this was edging dangerously close to verbal foreplay.

'You may have noticed that the royal *khanjar* has a pommel that is smaller than the rest.'

Was he teasing her?

'Oh…' Must she sound quite so disappointed?

'But it is heavily weighted and sharpened on both edges,' he went on, his lips tugging in the suspicion of a smile. 'It is infinitely more effective than other, inferior *khanjars*…'

'Ah…'

Or so relieved?

She thought for a moment. 'But if it's a royal *khanjar*, shouldn't it be larger than the rest?'

'Maybe I have another one I don't show everyone…'

Ah, again.

'I see,' she managed hoarsely.

'Why, Ms Michaels, I think you're flirting with me.'

'No, I'm not—' Casey's eyes cleared instantly, but before she had a chance to defend herself properly a guest appeared at Raffa's elbow.

'Ambassador, I'd like you to meet Ms Michaels, who has organised the auction for me this evening and is threatening to break all records…'

As he spoke Raffa gave Casey a look that made her tingle all over.

'Allow me to wish you every success, Ms Michaels,' the ambassador said, bowing low over Casey's hand.

The surprise at having her hand kissed didn't come close to Casey's surprise at the expression in Raffa's eyes. He was pleased at the honour paid to her by the ambassador, and yet he was uncomfortable with the other man touching her.

Raffa wanted her, Casey realised with a jolt, and was doing nothing to hide it. His fiercely appreciative look was daunting, and yet it made her feel empowered. Without her realising it he had given her confidence—something she had never thought to have.

It was good to be wanted. And to be wanted by a man she was already a little in love with was the most wonderful feeling on earth. She felt strong as a woman for the first time in her life.

But…

Could she finally live the fantasy? Casey wondered, stealing a look at Raffa. Could she sleep with him?

Her body responded eagerly to the thought, and the expression in Raffa's eyes as he met and held her gaze said anything was possible if she wanted it badly enough. And as his eyes warmed and his lips tugged with just the suggestion of shared humour she knew she did want it. She wanted Raffa to make love to her more than anything in the world.

Casey surprised everyone except Raffa and his team with the form her auction took. Instead of standing at the podium, which she would have found difficult, she played to her strengths as he had advised and ran a silent auction. It left all the billionaires guessing. There could be no public showing off, and instead all the bids had to be written down in secret.

The buzz in the ballroom was electric. Would this prince or that ambassador offer more than another? Surreptitious glances flew as people tried to guess what bid they would have to place in order to secure the most coveted objects, while envelopes with sealed bids inside were placed in the huge drum Casey had ready.

Perhaps only he could accurately predict that his fellow Sheikhs would err on the side of caution and offer extraordinary amounts, Raffa conjectured, rather than risk being pipped to the post by some inferior rival. Whatever— Casey had guessed it right.

And so the evening progressed, until a new drum was called for and even that was overflowing. Through it all Casey remained modest and charming, and in his eyes more beautiful than any other woman there as she hurried about the vast ballroom working as hard if not harder than any member of the team. She had excelled herself, thinking of everything—gold pens for men who normally had others to write for them, and sparkly crayons for the flock of spoiled princesses. And as he watched her he thought Casey possessed something far more valuable than money. The ability to instigate change for the better. She had displayed courage and determination in turning something so alien to her into a personal triumph.

'Running this event as a Dutch auction was a stroke of genius,' he told her bluntly when, after what seemed to him an unfeasibly long time, she returned to his side. Her face was flushed, and her eyes were sparking with success, and he had never seen her looking more beautiful.

'Thank you,' she said breathlessly. 'I think we've raised the record you were looking for, but I can't be sure until it's all been counted—there's so much of it.' She laughed, spreading her hands in innocent wonder that such wealth existed. 'There's a team working on it now. It's a real headache for them,' she confessed, 'trying to fathom out who has won what when some of the bids have so many noughts on them they have to count the numbers twice to be sure. And some of the shrewder individuals have even stooped to offering a mix of currencies to confuse the outcome,' she confided, as if she could not imagine greater shenanigans.

'Blackguards!' he exclaimed, taking her arm in his. He felt her immediate response to his touch and hoped she wouldn't find some reason to pull away. 'But I'm sure you'll work it out,' he said soothingly.

'I'm sure we will,' she agreed. 'And I really should get back to lend a hand…'

'Not yet.' He felt the tremor run through her as he held her gaze.

She blushed and looked away, but then said with touching sincerity, 'Just so long as we've done some good for your Bedouin project…'

'You've done more good than you know.'

'I'd like to think so,' she said softly.

'You will be the first to see the results of that. I promise you.' Even as he spoke he knew he *would* take her to the desert to see the truth of those words—for how else could he reward someone like Casey?

Raising her eyes, she looked at him, and as she slowly smiled he saw that not only had he regained her trust, but she had grown in confidence again, and that gave him more pleasure than he could safely express.

'You should be getting back to your guests,' she reminded him quietly.

'Yes,' he agreed, 'but then I'm going to take you home.'

She was instantly alert.

'Unless you don't want me to…?'

She stared at him for the longest time, and then said shyly, 'Thank you…I'd like that.'

'Go,' he murmured, touching her arm to urge her on. 'Go and enjoy your triumph, Casey Michaels. Tonight belongs to you…'

She had checked the pages of numbers so many times her eyes were blurring, but there was no mistake. They had raised a record amount of money—an astonishing amount of money—and she should be smiling. She wasn't smiling. She might be inexperienced, but she hoped her integrity was unquestioned. Even *she* had placed a bid for something she could afford at the auction—a pretty shawl, hand-woven by Bedouin weavers. She had been thrilled to find it overlooked in the feeding frenzy for so many more costly items.

Throwing her beautiful purchase around her shoulders, Casey pulled it close like a comfort blanket. It was softest alpaca, woven so fine it would have passed through a wedding ring. The colours of sky-blue and honey pleased and soothed her—but not enough for her to forget that the one person who could have purchased everything in the auction hadn't placed a single bid… Not enough for her to forget that her heart was broken, or that Raffa was not the man she had thought him.

Casey pulled herself together as members of the team clustered round to show her photographs of the latest mobile hospitals. She was determined to hide her feelings from everyone who had worked so hard alongside her. On the outside she was smiling, as they were, but inside she was cold with anger and disappointment—because Raffa, in his arrogance, had chosen not to donate a single penny to the scheme.

The trust between them was lost. The jolt out of her fantasy into reality was almost more than she could bear. Raffa had helped her grow in confidence to the point where sleeping with him had moved beyond an erotic fancy to a true desire for fulfillment. But now…

What hurt the most was that Raffa had made such a big deal out of her role in the auction. She wasn't looking for praise, just for him to take a personal interest and join in. Perhaps Sheikhs didn't do that. But it took a lot more than a bottomless pit of money to impress her. It was looking as if this event had been nothing more than a cynical exercise on Raffa's part—an entertainment to amuse the jaded palates of the rich. Had she really imagined she was falling in love with him? Had her body really responded with such excitement to every passing glance? She could never love a man like that.

'His Majesty is waiting, when you're ready,' one of Raffa's aides discreetly prompted.

Tumbled out of her reverie, Casey took a moment to respond. In the heat of her disappointment she had forgotten Raffa's promise to take her home. She had agreed to it before she had known he would remain coldly aloof whilst tempting his guests to empty their coffers in support of his good cause.

'Thank you,' she told the messenger politely. 'Would you please tell His Majesty that I have unexpectedly developed a headache and that I'm going straight home?'

The other helpers were already filing out of the room, and the man was clearly uncomfortable with the message she had given him to carry back to Raffa, but it couldn't be helped. There wasn't a prison cell grim enough to frighten her into sucking up to His Majesty Rafik al Rafar bin Haktari of A'Qaban.

The moment she was alone Casey scooped up the hem of her dress and checked around the room one last time, to be sure she was the last to leave and that everything was neatly put back in its place. She had barely made it through the door before she sensed a storm approaching—and at the head of that storm was a man...

She couldn't run in her shoes. Bending down to take them off, she realised it would take too much time and, kicking one off, she had to hobble away as best she could—with the ruler of A'Qaban in full hunter mode striding after her.

CHAPTER TEN

SHE'D had it with fairytales. Snapping Raffa an angry glance, Casey continued on to the exit, where she threw the door open and stumbled out into the night, leaving one shoe behind her.

Raffa followed moments later. Flinging the door wide, he caught hold of her within seconds. This was not the elegant, restrained Sheikh of the ballroom, but a fierce man stripped back to nature.

'What the hell is wrong with you?' Thrusting her up against the wall, he held her still with the weight of his body.

She whipped her face away with a sound of contempt.

'You'd better explain what's going on, Casey. I announced your name on the platform, and everyone in the ballroom is waiting to congratulate you. How could you come so far and let the team down now?'

The team? She went hot and cold all over, not having realised the enormity of what she'd done. 'I don't want praise!' she exclaimed, feeling angry and confused.

'No, you'd rather make a fool out of me and your team, who are standing on the stage right now, waiting for you.'

'I had no idea…'

'This isn't all about *you*, Casey.'

Her eyes filled at the accusation. 'I never thought it was. I—'

'So what *did* you think, Casey? That I was inviting you to share my bed tonight?'

She couldn't have felt more humiliated, and Raffa held her in front of him where there was no escape from his gaze.

'I thought as much,' he said softly.

Squeezing her eyes tightly shut, she turned away. Tears were threatening, and this was no time for a show of weakness; she had made herself look foolish enough as it was.

'I informed everyone that you were temporarily overwhelmed.' Raffa sounded distinctly unimpressed. 'I also told them that you would be back with us shortly, and that you would join your team to accept my congratulations.'

That was not a suggestion, Casey gathered, meeting an iron stare. 'You want to humiliate me,' she whispered.

'On the contrary,' Raffa said coldly. 'I want to thank you publicly for everything you and your team have done tonight.'

'And you, Raffa? What have *you* done tonight?'

'I don't know what you're talking about.'

'You didn't bid for anything. You didn't bid one single penny for any of the items on offer.'

'You should be flying high on your success at this moment,' he said firmly, 'and not worrying about what I did or didn't do.'

'I wish I could, but you've made it all seem pointless.'

'Because I didn't buy into your idea? Is that what you think?' His dark eyes scanned her face. 'Know this about me, Casey— I do what is right and not what is expected of me.'

'And I should be content with that?'

'You should trust me.'

'I don't know you, Raffa.' Still suffering what felt like terminal heartache, she jerked away. And only succeeded in stumbling on the step.

But Raffa caught her.

And slowly drew her close.

'I didn't do a thing,' he said.

'I know…' He was making a habit of that lately. She turned her face away, trying to remain immune to his persuasive warmth.

'Let me look,' he said, when she winced and tried not to put any weight on her shoeless foot.

'I'm fine.'

'Well, clearly you're not. Let me see, *habibi*.'

How could he call her sweetheart in Arabic after everything that had happened? This just wasn't fair. She stared at Raffa's outstretched hand suspiciously.

Slowly and reluctantly, she came to him. With the utmost care he bent her knee and lifted her tiny foot to examine it. Fortunately the sharp stone she must have trodden on had done no damage, but he massaged the sole of her foot, where the redness was showing, to ease any remaining discomfort.

'Better now?' he murmured, looking up.

'Better,' she admitted softly.

She sighed involuntarily and looked flustered—torn between believing the worst of him and wanting to be wrong, he guessed. Meantime she was forced to hang on to his shoulders to keep her balance, and he could feel her slender fingers shift slightly—as if she was tempted to explore further, and only her lack of experience married to her pride prevented it.

Standing up, he sensed the mood change between them; she had softened slightly. 'May I escort you back to the ballroom?' he suggested. 'But first you had better put this on.' He handed her the discarded shoe.

She looked at it, and then at him. Any comparisons to Cinderella would cost him dearly, he suspected. She tipped her chin and firmed her jaw. 'I'd better hurry,' she said, all business now. 'I've kept the team waiting long enough.'

He steadied her while she secured the strap on her shoe. He was proud of her, and proud of the team she had led, but there had to be easier women…

And he did easy now?

'Ready?' he said, calmly offering her his arm.

'Yes, I'm ready now.'

He felt the weight of her small hand on his arm as he held the door for her with his free hand. He liked that modest weight. He liked standing with Casey at the entrance to the ballroom until he was certain she had captured everyone's attention. And he liked the warm feeling inside him because he was so proud of her.

'Aren't you embarrassed, doing this?' she whispered as he led her forward.

'Embarrassed to be escorting my record-breaking employee to the stage, where she will receive her well-deserved acclaim? Why should I be embarrassed?'

He stood back while Casey and her team received everyone's thanks. They had raised a phenomenal amount of money in the shortest imaginable time, and it pleased him even more to see Casey standing back to urge her colleagues forward. She was more like him than she knew—a thought that under other circumstances might have amused him, but tonight made him regret the fact that very shortly he would have to turn his attention fully to ruling his country and this interlude with Casey Michaels must come to an end.

But not yet, he thought as she prepared to leave the stage—not now, when she had grown so much in confidence. Because that opened up a whole raft of possibilities.

'Remember you're leaving with me,' he murmured discreetly as he escorted her off the stage.

There might have been an electric charge beneath his hand, and the air was certainly electric between them as he adjusted her shawl. It was the pretty shawl fate had tempted her to bid for that night.

'Or perhaps you'd rather take a cab?' he said, noticing how she trembled when his breath brushed her neck.

'I'm sure there will be plenty,' she retorted, staring him steadily in the eyes. 'Raffa, you have to stop teasing me like this. If I'm going to work in A'Qaban you must let me do things for myself.'

'*Are* you going to work here, Casey?'

She fell quiet, and he guessed she was still confused. She thought him arrogant. She hadn't forgiven him for his supposedly miserly actions that night.

'That's in your hands, Raffa,' she said at last.

'Maybe you will. But I'd like you to come somewhere with me before I make you an offer, and before you decide whether to take it or not.'

'Come with you where?' she said suspiciously.

'Let's find out, shall we?' he murmured, taking hold of her arm.

He waved his guards away, wanting Casey to himself. He kept on walking until they reached a long, silent corridor, at the end of which some double doors led on to impressive formal gardens. It would be difficult, if not impossible for Casey to remain tense and angry here. As he'd expected, she stopped and gazed around, forgetting her anger and confusion as she took in their surroundings.

'Raffa, this is beautiful…'

The scent of strawberry *sheesha* smoke was in the air, and fountains played tinkling background music. Even he, who had seen this many times before, paused to appreciate the elaborate mosaics and lush green planting. The architects he had employed to make his vision a reality had exceeded his wildest dreams. As had Casey, he reflected wryly.

Taking her hands, he said, 'I want to add my personal thanks to the guests' for what you did tonight. You can't imagine how many people will benefit from the money you raised.'

'Then I'm pleased…' Her voice faded and her gaze dropped as she remembered her disappointment.

He drew her closer.

'Raffa…' She placed a hand against his chest, but she didn't press very hard, and then her fingers curled around the edges of his robe. 'I wish…'

He didn't let her get any further. Perhaps it was the tears in her eyes, or the trembling of her lips, but he was overwhelmed by the need to reassure her.

Tasting her was tasting heaven. Holding her against him was an education in everything he'd been missing. He deepened the kiss and felt a surge of desire when she responded, and he went on kissing her until Casey's reluctance was transformed into whimpering sighs.

But then his sane side took over. What was he doing? Where was this going? There was only one possible destination, and he would never take advantage of Casey while she was tired and confused and so vulnerable. Kissing the corner of her mouth, he pulled back. Bringing out his phone, he summoned his limousine, and then, taking her by the hand, he led her back through the doors.

The limousine was at the kerb. Knowing she was tired, he supported her arm so she wouldn't stumble. 'My driver will take you home.'

Her eyes cleared and she stared at him in bewilderment. Gradually the realisation came to her that the kiss had been a kiss, and nothing more.

'Goodnight, Casey,' he murmured, handing her safely into the car.

She turned to stare back at him through the rear window. He shouldn't have been surprised to see the anger and confusion in her eyes, but whatever he had chosen to do for the auction, whatever his reasons for drawing back from wanting to make love to Casey, wasn't anyone's business but his own.

As soon as breakfast had been delivered the following morning she went back to bed and hid her head under the pillow. What she thought that would achieve Casey had no idea. The day had to be faced, even if the night before had been the utmost in humiliation. Tossing her pillow to the floor, she sat up crosslegged on the bed. Touching her fingertips to her mouth, where Raffa's sharp black stubble had abraded her, she realised her lips were still tender and swollen from his kiss.

His kiss…

Closing her eyes, she relived every moment of the embrace, quivering with arousal. And quickly jerked herself round. Sometimes her body frightened her. The way it reacted so violently to thoughts of Raffa—as if it knew something she didn't—was truly alarming.

With a sigh, she shook her head, forced to accept that nothing, not even her own fear of intimacy, could stop her wanting him.

Leaping out of bed, she stood hugging herself as she thought things through. How bad did Raffa have to be for this longing to go away? He was no good for her. He lived his life behind a guarded façade, thinking money was the answer to everything. But when the chips were down...

She didn't want to think about the auction. And she had to eat to get through the day. She looked at the delicious food and juices waiting on the table. Maybe if she ate breakfast...maybe if she went through the motions of a normal day...her heart wouldn't ache so much and she could screw her business head back on.

She was so tense by the time she sat down at the table she didn't even notice the fabulous view over the marina and the pearlescent ocean beyond. Having poured a cup of fresh mint tea, she unfurled a copy of that morning's *A'Qaban Times*—and got no further than the headline.

Last bid opened is from ruling Sheikh, who promises to double record-breaking auction proceeds.

A groan escaped Casey's throat. Putting the paper down, she pushed her plate away and stood up. Suddenly she wasn't hungry any more.

Raffa was on the polo field, his office told her.

She didn't have an outfit for polo, but she did have her various purchases stowed in the wardrobe. Selecting the modest skirt and cardigan she had bought for work, along with her low heeled office shoes, she decided on no make-up and hair tied back. This was not an outing but a penance, and perhaps the last appointment she would ever have with Raffa. She had been far too quick to jump to conclusions.

But he had thrown money at the auction rather than taking part, Casey reflected in the hotel limousine on the way to the polo field. That being the case, once she had made this apology she wasn't sure they had much left to say to each other. How Raffa lived his life was no business of hers, but somehow she had imagined them being close in a place where all the jewels and couture clothes in the world made no difference. And now she had to face the fact that wasn't so.

CHAPTER ELEVEN

CASEY wasn't sure quite what to do when she arrived at the polo field. Seeing as the hotel driver was instantly recognised by the security guards, she decided it was best to ask him to take her as far as he could to avoid any run-ins with Raffa's bodyguards.

Having thanked the driver, Casey left the car and walked up to the fence bordering the field of play, where she stood leaning over it. The match had already started, and her gaze was immediately drawn to Raffa. Wearing pale breeches and a dark shirt, he had a ferocious-looking face-guard in place and was altogether a formidable sight. She remembered reading somewhere that a polo ball could travel at up to a hundred miles an hour—which explained the guard, as well as the chunky leather knee protectors strapped to his legs.

Legs which were currently wrapped around the quivering flanks of a sweating mare. She was transfixed by his strength and control. If she hadn't been half in love with him already, Raffa at full gallop, wielding a mallet with such remarkable skill, would have been enough. She moved closer, drawn in by the speed and power of the game and wanting to speak to him when he dismounted in the paddock at the end of the chukka.

As he pulled off his helmet and ruffled his thick black hair, he confirmed her opinion that in close-fitting breeches Raffa was prodigious in every sense of the word. She blushed self-consciously when he glanced her way. Having weighed up the leggy blondes hanging round him, though, she decided her apology must wait.

'Excuse me, Ms Michaels?'

She started guiltily, finding a security guard standing at her shoulder. 'I'm sorry, I don't have a pass,' she hurried to explain. 'But I do work for His Majesty.'

The man waited until she had finished before politely informing her that His Majesty had asked him to escort her to the pavilion, where she could sit in the shade.

'Oh, I see…' Casey smiled and relaxed, and then glanced anxiously towards Raffa, who was busy checking on his polo pony and didn't see her looking.

A shady pavilion would be just the place for him to fire her, Casey reflected.

Or he might just be being considerate, her sensible inner voice suggested, as the sun was blazing down.

Thanking the messenger, she followed the man towards the large marquee. She paused on the threshold, seeing it was full of noisy, confident people—the sort of people she designed campaigns for but never mixed with.

'Ms Michaels?' the man escorting Casey prompted.

She couldn't keep him waiting, Casey reasoned. Bracing herself, she walked inside.

The interior of the tent was the epitome of luxury, with large squashy sofas upholstered in cream linen, and any number of easy chairs gathered around low, pale wood tables. The whole area was temperature controlled, and there were beautiful flower arrangements everywhere. There was even a bar and a buffet, with waiter service.

Stepping over colourful rugs, she was tempted to linger by plump cushions whose pattern reminded her of her beautiful auction purchase. In bolder colours, perhaps, the cushions boasted the same intricate pattern as her shawl. There was even a giant screen on which to watch the match, though the game was taking place only a few yards away.

It seemed most of Raffa's guests preferred to collect around the bar and the buffet table, in small, tight-knit intimate groups, Casey noticed, deciding she would keep to herself. But she was soon restless. She wanted to see the match—and not on a giant screen.

'Would it be possible for me to watch the match outside the pavilion?' she asked the guard before he left.

'Not on the screen in here?' He seemed surprised.

What was the point in that? Casey wondered. When she could watch it just as well on a screen in her hotel room? 'I'd prefer to sit outside, if it's not too much trouble for you…'

'No trouble at all,' the man said. 'But the sun is very strong.' Sensing her disappointment, he added, 'Perhaps if we put a chair for you beneath the awning you would still be in the shade, as His Majesty has requested…'

The last thing she wanted was to get this man in trouble with Raffa. 'If His Majesty won't think you went against his orders, that would be perfect; thank you.'

A large chair was brought and positioned for her in the shade, where she still had a clear view of the field. She perched tensely on the edge of it, conscious that Raffa was already well into the next chukka. Glancing at the scoreboard, she saw that his side was winning by one goal. She watched him marshalling his troops as the other side drew even. His grim determination to win was obvious as he turned his pony in tight, tense circles. The members of his team responded instantly, seeming to draw themselves up in the saddle and firm their resolve.

Raffa was a king amongst men, and one who didn't need a title to prove it, but still she feared for his safety and tensed as the air horn blew and the game restarted.

How could she relax, knowing Raffa was in danger? Her apology, difficult though that would be, was the least of her fears. Watching the riders heading for each other at full tilt, whilst swinging their mallets like deadly weapons, made her flinch each time one of them came close to Raffa.

Minutes passed while hooves thundered a tattoo on the sun-baked ground. Perhaps the most frightening thing of all was that she could sense what Raffa meant to do. It was as if they were on the same wavelength, thinking the same thoughts. She was no horse rider, but what he planned seemed utter madness to her.

Riding at full stretch, he leaned over the neck of his pony and with infinite precision swung his mallet to secure another goal. Realising she was biting her knuckles, Casey made herself sit back. This was the time to relax, while the teams changed ends—which they did after every goal.

How she wished for a world in which she and the ruler of A'Qaban were not at odds, Casey reflected, aching with tension as the air horn sounded. Raffa had a handicap of ten, which was the highest possible ranking in the game, and she had read that only one man in the world could match him. For all that, she was still gripped by a prescient dread that something would go wrong today. She must feel that way, Casey reasoned, because Raffa would never back down, however tough a fight became.

Thankfully, half time arrived without incident, though Casey shrank back in her chair as everyone from the marquee hurried outside. The end of the half was the cue for spectators to either head over to the paddock, where the polo players were gathered, or onto the field to stamp the divots down. Casey chose the latter, selecting a small patch of ground in front of the marquee on which to exercise her frustration at drawing so many wrong conclusions where Raffa was concerned.

The tip-tap of iron on the paved yard alerted her to fresh ponies being led round by the stable lads. A bell rang, signalling it was time for the riders to mount up and for everyone else to clear the field. As she watched the teams prepare, Casey offered up a silent plea that Raffa would remain unharmed in the second half. He sprang into the saddle, ignoring the attempt of a beautiful young girl to hold his stirrup for him, preferring to adjust his own equipment, Casey noticed with relief.

And there was rather a lot of equipment to adjust, Casey also noticed, beginning to wish she hadn't looked.

Raffa flashed a glance her way, emphasising how closely tuned they were. It was a disturbing moment for Casey, as well as a reminder to keep her head clear of questionable thoughts for the remaining three chukkas.

Raffa was gone in a rattle of hooves, leaving Casey too agitated to watch the second half from her seat in the shade. She approached the fence bordering the field of play and leaned over it. She didn't like failure any more than Raffa, she accepted, flinching back as Raffa thundered past to steal a ball, but were they too far apart in the things that mattered for them ever to work successfully together?

In Raffa's world, she concluded, money talked. Whereas in her world it paid bills. He had thrown colossal sums of money at the auction while she had been hoping for some small personal gesture, she realised now.

She couldn't knock him, what he'd done was great, but she had always been a romantic dreamer. But why should Raffa change any more than she could change her own frigid ways?

Casey was still mulling this over when she heard a shout. Starting back in alarm, she realised Raffa's horse was galloping straight for her—and it was him shouting at her to get out of the way.

Raffa was almost flat on his horse's neck as he pressed it to the limit, but as the drumming hooves beat a deadly tattoo Casey's legs remained wooden and unresponsive. Raffa was trying to ride another man off the field, she saw in horror.

No, the other man's horse was out of control, and Raffa was trying to push it off course because it was bolting straight for her.

Shoulder to shoulder, knee to knee, Raffa and the other polo player bore down on her. She was certain they were going to ride straight over her when Raffa swerved at the last minute, somehow avoiding a collision with the fence. The other rider didn't possess half his skill, and she screamed soundlessly as horse, rider and fence hurtled towards her.

CHAPTER TWELVE

CASEY barely registered what happened next. One moment she was watching the impending disaster play out, feet refusing to budge and brain refusing to compute what was happening, and the next she was high off the ground and safe in Raffa's arms. 'You saved my life,' she managed weakly as he settled her on the saddle in front of him.

Grim-faced, Raffa remained silent as he tightened his grip around her waist.

Strength gone, she folded into him. 'Is the other horse okay?'

'And the rider,' he informed her tersely. 'The fence didn't make it.'

She turned her head. The sight of Raffa's strong white teeth gritted behind his face guard brought back every second of the drama in heart-stopping slow motion—the fierce cry from his throat and the blaze of his eyes as he raced to sweep her out of danger.

'Thank you...' It was so inadequate.

'Please try to remain still until I have you checked over.' Raffa urged his polo pony towards the first aid tent. 'You little fool,' he murmured in a low-pitched voice stretched tight with tension. 'Why did you put yourself in danger?'

Because I was watching you, worrying about you...caring about you...

She knew Raffa didn't expect an answer—not that she was

incapable of giving him one. She could do more than rest against him like a newborn baby, with all her strength gone and no will of her own.

Shock, Casey registered groggily, willing it to pass quickly.

'I get you out of the sun only for you to decide it's time to hug a fence. Can't I leave you alone for a minute?'

Once again, no answer was required, Casey registered as Raffa's rough cheek accidentally brushed her face. She sensed he held himself responsible for the accident, and was going to remain in this severe mood for some time. 'It wasn't your fault. It was all my fault.'

'We'll discuss your part in this later.'

'Did we win?'

'We survived,' he said dryly. Reining in by the first aid tent, he tossed the reins to a waiting stable lad. Swinging down from the saddle, he reached up. 'Come,' he said in a suddenly much kinder voice, 'lean on me…'

He lowered her with infinite care, but as she reached the ground her knees buckled. 'Watch out!' Raffa exclaimed, catching hold of her.

'Sorry…' She was still faint with shock—but not so faint she didn't know when the ruler of A'Qaban had swung her into his arms and was carrying her safely the rest of the way.

The nurse pronounced Casey fit and well; Raffa pronounced her fate.

'As I can't leave you alone for a minute,' he said, 'I'm going to keep you with me while you're in A'Qaban.'

It was all she had ever wanted to hear, but Raffa made it sound like a punishment. Still, when you were confidently expecting an airline ticket home, anything else was a reprieve, Casey reminded herself, brushing her clothes down as they left the first aid tent together.

'I'll be travelling into the interior after the trophy for this match has been awarded.'

As she exclaimed with pleasure he dampened her enthusiasm. 'I can make no allowances for the accident, Casey. You do understand that, don't you?'

'Yes,' she said tensely.

'The interior of A'Qaban is dangerous territory where shocks are commonplace—'

'I understand.' More dangerous than a polo field?

'Your powers of recovery from this are crucial. If an accident happens in the desert you can't waste time, you must think immediately: what next?'

That was exactly what she *was* thinking.

'So, are you up for it?'

'You won't be disappointed. I'll do everything you expect me to and more.'

'But…?' Raffa's eyes narrowed, sensing there was something else she wanted to say.

Casey drew a deep breath. 'But I came to apologise…for last night. I read the papers this morning, and—'

'That's something I don't want to discuss with you,' Raffa said, frowning.

'But—'

'No buts. My decisions aren't up for discussion. You're still in the running for this job. That's all you should care about. But only if you can concentrate and be ready to leave your hotel within the hour.'

'I will be,' she said steadily.

Raffa arrived at the hotel in a rugged Jeep with no outriders and no bodyguards in attendance—at least none she could see. Casey was waiting on the steps, as instructed, dressed as a storm trooper once more, though not feeling so odd as when she had arrived at A'Qaban airport, because this time she was dressed in a way Raffa approved of for the desert. She had made one change—replacing her ugly hat with the lightweight shawl she'd bought at the auction, wrapping it around her head and shoulders in the A'Qabani fashion. It was a sensible choice, because it gave her the option of drawing it over her nose and mouth if the air grew dusty.

Swinging out of the driver's seat, he took hold of her backpack. He too was dressed in survival gear, though his clothes looked considerably more worn than hers.

'Sun cream?' he rapped.

'Of course.'

'I see you're wearing my *atija*; that's a sensible precaution.'

'Your…?'

'*Atija* means gift,' he explained, opening the door of the Jeep for her. 'The shawl was my personal gift to the auction. Now, get in.'

She was still fingering the fine material as she absorbed what Raffa had said. Her shawl was his gift to the auction…his small, *thoughtful* gift to the auction. On top of all the fabulous jewels he had donated, he had given something he liked, something that was representative of the traditional craft of his country. It was everything she had hoped he might do; everything she had so firmly believed he hadn't done.

'Come on,' he said impatiently, bouncing her into action, 'The people of the desert don't wait for anyone—they obey nature's rules, rather than man's.'

'Are you Bedouin?' she asked as she climbed into the Jeep.

'My mother was a Bedouin princess.'

And that conjured up the most wonderful images. She longed to know more, but there was a reserve in Raffa's voice that told her to leave it. If Raffa didn't want to discuss his parents with her, she respected that.

'There's a first aid kit here, and water here.' He pointed them out to her when they were both safely strapped in. 'And we have a radio as well as a satellite phone, should we need them. There's also a tracking device on the Jeep, so that we know where we are and my people know too.'

A frisson of fear mixed with Casey's excitement. Her fantasies were left behind as she faced the realities of the desert. Raffa was warning her that they were going into dangerous terrain where anything could happen. She had prepared well. She had even taken a first aid course before leaving England. She knew how to handle a radio and was ready for anything.

Except for riding on horseback.

'You're joking!' Casey exclaimed when Raffa drew up after an hour of driving.

'I never joke,' Raffa informed her. 'Or at least I don't employ humour out here, where jokes cost lives.'

A'Qabani handlers were standing by a horse transporter, while two horses were tethered in the shade. The real road had petered out, and in front of them lay miles of unseen desert. Casey gazed down the dusty trail, hardly able to believe she was about to embark on her first real expedition on horseback. When she turned back to Raffa he was winding yards of black cloth around his head.

'We call it a *howlis*,' he explained, throwing the ties over his shoulder.

He looked amazing, with just a slit for his expressive black eyes.

'The closest word you have to describe it would be a turban. It keeps the sun off my face and the dust out of my eyes, nose, ears and mouth.'

And makes you look stunning along the way, Casey thought, nodding sagely. This was not a turban. A turban was respectable headgear. This was a wild man's bandanna-cum-scarf that made Raffa look like a brigand. His expression was hidden, which she didn't like, but his eyes—those she did like. They might have been amused as he stared at, or then again not. She could decide. Her throat dried as she watched him stride towards the horses, and then she saw the men bring out a mule loaded with provisions and her mouth dried a little more. This was going to be some expedition.

Excited as she was, she felt a tremble of alarm. What did it mean, this trek into the desert? She was prepared in the practical sense, but in another, far more personal sense, was she ready for this? Was she ready for the untamed desert with an untamed man? What did she really think was going to happen when she was out there with Raffa, miles away from anyone, and from convention and civilisation?

She was terrified, but excited too. She was ready to face most challenges, and Raffa was the biggest challenge of all. He was so much more complex than his forward publicity had suggested. He was also the most rampantly masculine man she had ever encountered, and yet he was so strongly principled she felt safe with him; safer than she had ever felt with a man before. He was a protector and would keep her safe. Virginally safe? She pressed her lips together and sighed; that was an unknown.

'Are you coming?' he called, before she could get herself worked up about it.

Raffa was holding her mount and looking her way. She had no idea what he was thinking.

That element of the uncertain, the unknown, that she had always been groping towards, was hers for the taking—if she had the courage. And actually, right at this moment, she was more frightened of the sweet-looking little pony Raffa was patting than Raffa. The last time she had been on a saddle was on a donkey at the beach when she had been a very little girl.

'Come on, he won't bite,' Raffa encouraged.

She had to admit the dapple grey did look kind. The gelding was decked out with a fancy harness and a colourful saddle cloth to protect its sturdy back from her. And at least she didn't have to ride Raffa's horse—a jet-black, impatient looking stallion, with a fierce stare like its master. The monster mount was currently tossing its head and chomping at its bit in impatience.

'Ready?' Raffa encouraged. 'How else do you think we're going to get to our destination?'

She'd rather walk.

'If you don't hurry I'll put you on the mule and tie your backpack to the horse.'

Okay. Deep breath. So she'd ride the horse. How hard could it be?

Very hard.

She fell stiff-legged off her mount the moment they stopped, after what felt like hours of bone-jouncing trekking. They had reached an oasis around which a tented city had formed.

Casey remained where she fell, hugging her knees and silently yowling at the pain in her limbs. At least it gave her chance to admire the scenery, she reasoned as Raffa shook his head, slowly unwinding his *howlis* as he looked down at her.

She needed some immediate distraction from that sort of wow. Well, there was plenty of distraction around. They were on top of a sand dune, from where they could look down at the rolling desert painted in shades of ochre and umber. The plateau was punctuated by a limpid lilac lake fringed by shades of green. The oasis not only provided a lifeline to the wandering people who used it, but to the local wildlife, Casey saw, spotting desert gazelles grown brave enough to come and drink in the failing light.

Rolling over onto her stomach, she exclaimed softly as she watched them, forgetting her own discomfort. It was just such a magical sight—timid creatures finding courage as she had in the desert, beneath a sky that was slowly turning from palest aqua to midnight-blue, while at the horizon it was shot through with dazzling scarlet.

'Get up,' Raffa rapped, putting an end to her idyll. 'There are scorpions in this area.'

With a shriek, she leapt up, slapping her sides energetically.

'Remember to check your boots each time you put them on,' he told her sternly—one instruction she was unlikely to forget.

'Is this the end of our journey?' she asked, still shuddering as she hurried after him.

'It could be—for you.'

'For me?'

'If you find a scorpion in your clothes.'

That did it. With a shriek that startled the gazelles, she whacked herself all over while Raffa held the back of his neck, viewing her contortions with a puzzled frown. 'With all that stuff in your backpack,' he said, 'didn't you remember to bring some bug spray?'

'I could be dead by the time I find it.'

'Okay, relax. Even the biggest scorpions you'll find round here would only sting you like a wasp.'

'Nice,' she accused him.

'Would you like me to search you?'

'Absolutely not,' she exclaimed, springing away. 'So why are we here?' she demanded, all fired up now.

'I thought you might like to see how the money you raised will be spent.'

As he walked away she chased after him. 'Raffa, wait... thank you.'

Out of breath, she rested, hands on knees, at the foot of the next dune.

'Why are you thanking me?' His cheek creased attractively as he smiled.

She straightened up. 'You haven't even allowed me to apologise to you yet.'

'For success?'

'Raffa, wait.' She gazed up with frustration as his panther stride increased the distance between them. How was it she slipped two steps back for every step she tried to take up the dune?

Thankfully, Raffa had paused on the brow of the hill to stare down at her.

'I'll be right there,' she called up. In maybe a year, the rate she was going.

'Here, let me help you,' he said, leaning down. Grabbing her wrist, he pulled her up by sheer brute force. 'Turn your feet out a little,' he advised. 'Think of the sand as snow. You can even side-step if you find that easier.'

'You ski?'

'Of course.'

Of course.

And, actually, she rather liked being helpless for once, and having him drag her up.

Close to, the tented city was a revelation. It was laid out neatly around the oasis, which flamed crimson where the grey water had harnessed the last solar gasp of the day. Camels and ponies and mules were gathered in a shady corral, and the voices of children carried shrilly towards them on the night breeze.

'Come on,' Raffa said, more relaxed than she'd ever seen him. 'I want to introduce you.'

Casey stared at his outstretched hand. Was there a difference in taking hold of Raffa's hand because she wanted to and taking hold of it because she had to, because without his help she was stranded on the sand?

This was not a time to get philosophical, Casey concluded as he looked at her impatiently.

She made a grab for it, and screamed as Raffa dragged her with him in a pell-mell race down the sand dune. He swung her into his arms at the bottom of it so she wouldn't fall over.

'You brute,' she exclaimed, laughing as she tried to catch her breath. 'You really scared me.'

'Did I?'

He was wholly unrepentant, and the children were laughing, forming a circle around them. Impulsively, Casey reached for one small hand and Raffa reached for another, and before they knew it there was one big circle and they were dancing round and round beneath a rising crescent moon—for no other reason than they were all so happy.

The children led them deeper into the encampment, where everything was orderly and looked so permanent Casey had to remind herself that appearances could be deceptive. Her gaze strayed to Raffa at this point, who always managed to look like the baddest man on the planet, but who right now was listening to a little girl read her favourite book.

The Bedouin would be moving on soon, she realised, taking the moon and the sun as their guide and accepting no boundaries other than those raised by nature. It was a privilege to be able to spend time with them. It was a gift from Raffa, and the only gift she wanted.

Having this chance to visit the community the auction had helped, to see the travelling school and the medical facilities, made everything clearer to Casey. Minor niggles in her own life were suddenly immaterial. Anything she could do would never be enough to repay the friendship of these people. As the children led her by the hand to show her their prized pencils and blocks of writing paper, she felt humbled, and in that moment determined to open her eyes and see what else there was in the big, complex world she inhabited, outside her own small corner of it.

CHAPTER THIRTEEN

'HUNGRY?' Raffa queried when they had completed their tour of the camp.

'Starving,' Casey admitted.

'Shall we make some food together?'

She took a step back and then realised he was serious. 'Okay…but no sheep's eyes.' Remembering Raffa's humour, she wasn't taking any chances.

'No sheep's eyes,' he conceded dryly, wiping his face on the unwound black cloth of the *howlis* he was now wearing slung around his neck.

So he was gorgeous, she accepted, taking in the luminous black gaze and thick, inky-black hair. Super-gorgeous, she amended when he smiled.

'Is this your tent?' she asked as he led her towards one of the larger pavilions.

Ruffling his wild hair, Raffa shook his head. 'I don't own anything in the desert. Think of it as the ocean,' he said, ducking his head to lift the flap away from the entrance for her. 'Like all other the voyagers in this vast wilderness, I use what I need and pass on what is left. I add what I can for the next traveler.'

'You make it sound like a guardian angel system,' Casey observed.

'That's exactly what it is.'

Where was *her* guardian angel? Casey wondered, hesitating

on the threshold of the tent. She needed advice badly. She dearly wanted to find out all she could about A'Qaban's people and their culture, and she desperately wanted to know everything about Raffa. But now they were alone, if he should…If he…

Wringing her hands in agitation, she knew she'd make a mess of things. She'd spoil things—change everything. She couldn't have just a night with a man like Raffa and then pick up and carry on as if nothing had happened.

And if he didn't make a move—

'Casey?' he prompted. 'Are you coming? I want to get on.'

'Give me a moment…I'm just drinking it all in.' Not to mention engaging in a war of the worlds with her doubt demons.

As Raffa disappeared inside the tent, Casey thought about him with the little girl—how gentle and tender he'd been as he'd listened to the child reading her story. She thought of the fun they'd both had with the children when they'd first arrived. Raffa wasn't some unfeeling oaf who would tumble her on the cushions and have his evil way, he was a cultured, confident, caring individual.

So what was she going to do? In the absence of a guardian angel, a decision was required.

'Come on,' he called impatiently.

She was still hesitating when he appeared at her elbow. He'd come back for her and he wasn't about to take no for an answer.

Casey stood entranced inside the Bedouin tent. It was more comfortably furnished than many hotel rooms. Heaps of cushions in rich homespun textures spoke of months of dedicated weaving, while there were hand-woven rugs on the floor and hangings on the walls in muted jewel colours. The space was illuminated by a brass lantern fixed to a central post, and the tempting aroma of hot sweet coffee was in the air, along with some spice—incense, maybe. The actual walls of the pavilion were made of dark, heavy, leathery material.

'Camel hide,' Raffa explained, when she stroked her hand across it. 'Nothing is wasted here.'

'I can see that,' she agreed, viewing two horn goblets on a low, gleaming brass table. 'This is absolutely amazing…just like Aladdin's cave.'

'Ah, *Ala-ad-din*,' he said. 'We have that story too.'

'So you know both versions?' She turned from her examination of a large, decorative vase, hungry for more knowledge of Raffa.

'I was brought up and educated in England, but my nanny was careful to introduce me to the culture of both countries.'

Another gem of knowledge she locked away. Some might think Raffa had enjoyed a richer start in life than most, but he had just reminded her that he had known his fair share of tragedy too.

'So what do you think of A'Qaban now you have left the glamour of the city behind?' he said, distracting her from her thoughts.

'I love it. I'm constantly surprised.'

'Live with us and then judge us?' he murmured, slanting Casey an amused look. 'In our language we would say, *Ashirna wa akhbirna*.'

She tried the unfamiliar words with Raffa's encouragement, which naturally meant she had to look at his lips. Well, it was important to see the shapes he was making—luscious, all of them.

He turned from her momentarily and grew still. He was listening and evaluating the deeper sound of parents' voices outside providing a counterpoint to their shrill-voiced children, she realised, and only when he was sure all was well did he relax. The bad-boy sheikh conjured up by the tabloid press was nowhere to be seen. That character was a chimera, a smoke-screen for the man Raffa was in private. Raffa was a natural-born protector, not a playboy, and in spite of the vast power and wealth he wielded he was a man of simple tastes; a man so far removed from his public persona it was hard to believe she had ever been gullible enough to judge this particularly interesting book by its cover.

'Do you recognise these?' he said, pointing to some cushions. They were arranged around a low, hammered brass table, and had a familiar pattern. It was the same pattern as her shawl, Casey realised with a thrill of discovery. 'They're beautiful,' she said, 'just like this.' As she spoke, she stroked the filmy folds of her shawl. 'I love my shawl and I won't be parted from it…' Let him make what he would out of that.

He handled the revelation Casey had made coolly. Things were moving rapidly onto another level between them and he didn't want to force the issue. He had brought Casey to the desert to introduce her to his people, but behind that intention were his growing feelings towards her. When she'd first arrived, so gauche and shy, and vulnerable in his presence, he couldn't have considered anything other than a business relationship. But as her confidence had come to the fore, and she'd grown in self-belief as a woman, other possibilities had opened up.

They had established much while saying little, he reflected, thinking how lovely she looked in the shawl—and that was the way of the desert people. Casey had many of the qualities he most admired in the Bedouin. Small things made and given with love meant more to her than all the jewels in his strong room, and it pleased him more than he could say to think she had picked out the shawl above everything else he had donated to the auction. What she could not have known was that he had intended to buy her anything she wanted—anything she had made an unsuccessful bid for in thanks for organising the event. Casey had made that unnecessary by selecting the one item no one else had seen any value in.

'I'll light a fire so we can star-gaze while we eat,' he suggested, knowing she would enjoy that.

'Could I bathe first? I mean…' She blushed as he turned to look at her. 'I'm all gritty after the ride. Is it safe to swim in the oasis?'

'Perfectly safe. It's shallow and warm, and there is firm

sand underfoot. You should have it to yourself at this time of night. Why don't I go down there first, to take a swim and scout it out for you?'

'Would you do that?'

At this moment in time he would do anything for her. 'I'll lay the fire first, so that you're warm, and if you sort out the food we brought we'll decide what to do with it when we've finished our swim.'

'We brought food to cook?'

'We have a mule,' he reminded her dryly. 'Don't you remember the saddle bags?'

'Ah, yes…I thought they were—' She shook her head. 'I don't know what I thought they were.'

'Well, now you know. They hold your gourmet supper—that's if you can cook.'

She laughed, and he thought her lovely, and he held her gaze long after they had both stopped smiling at each other. It was the first time they had been so relaxed in each other's company, with the façade of who they were and what they expected from each other stripped away. But then Casey's smile faded as if she realised how intimate this was becoming.

'Don't be long,' she said shyly, turning away.

'You'll be safe here,' he said, touching her arm.

She smiled—a little tremulously, he thought, and he wanted the confident woman back. He wanted Casey to enjoy life to the full and know how valuable she was—not just as a colleague in business, but as a human being.

To that end there must be no more desire-charged looks or testosterone running riot, he told himself as he lifted the lid of an intricately carved Iroko chest. 'You'll find fresh clothes in here.' He helped himself to a new black robe without turning round to face her. 'Take whatever you need.'

She didn't answer, and he guessed she was still taking stock of her position. She was alone in the desert with him, with attraction gaining momentum every minute as they got to know each other better. He would make love to her here, in the most beautiful and challenging place on earth. He had wanted to make love to Casey from the moment they met, but would only do so when he was certain she felt unthreatened and safe in every way.

Then there would only be one danger left, he reflected, which was Casey's sexual appetite. It had been repressed for so long that when she finally let go he had a feeling it would consume her. But when that happened he would be ready.

'I've got Halloumi cheese, mango, pine nuts and some green stuff in those saddle bags—so get thinking,' he told her lightly on the way out of the tent. 'I'm hungry,' he added with a casual shrug, as if his stomach was the only part of his body making demands on him these days, 'and I'm sure you are too…'

She looked relieved, as he'd hoped she would, as she started to work out her menu, while he badly needed to work off some energy. Slinging a towel over his shoulder, he headed at speed for the calming waters of the oasis.

She had the ingredients neatly lined up and a plan in her head by the time Raffa returned from his swim. 'All clear at the oasis,' he called to her from outside the tent. 'You can have your swim in absolute privacy while I find some more tinder for our fire.'

She would have liked to have seen him in the simple black robes, but he had taken them with him and her imagination had to do the rest. She waited until he had gone, and then peeped out of the tent to be sure it was all clear. She had dreamed of this moment, and ran down to the oasis as fast as she could, with the sort of abandonment she hadn't felt since she was a child, when a swim had meant plunging into an icy river. This was very different. She paused at the brink, just to stare for a moment at the beauty of the desert all around her. She had the moonlight to herself, and the stars were twinkling…

Strangely, she felt quite safe—the Raffa effect, she guessed. Though remembering his warning about bugs, she checked around first before leaving her clothing on a rock. She had intended to leave her underwear on, but at the last moment she decided to take it off and rinse it through for the next day. She was quite alone— not that she needed an excuse to go skinny-dipping.

Stepping into the water, she cautiously made her way forward. Raffa had been right. The ground beneath her feet felt firm and there were no pebbles underfoot. The water had been heated to body temperature by the desert sun and, guessing this would be the most magical thing she had ever done, she launched herself in. Putting her head down, she began to swim seriously.

It was some time later when she remembered she was supposed to be helping Raffa prepare a meal. It was just so hard to tear herself away from the oasis…

Lifting her head to get her bearings, she saw a tall, robed figure watching her from the bank. She swam to shore, while Raffa came down from the dune where he'd been standing guard to meet her. He was just a few feet away as she crouched self-consciously in the shallows. His face was shadowed by the *howlis*, which he had put on again with his robe, and his eyes were bright in the darkness.

There was a brief flash of white as he smiled. 'Did you forget something?' he murmured.

For a moment she wondered what he meant, but then she realised that in her excitement she had run down to the oasis without a towel. 'Did you bring one?'

Raffa's answer was to open his arms to her.

Would she trust him enough to come out of the water? The moment was as crucial for him as it was for Casey. Sexual frustration was eating him up from the inside out.

He waited on the bank until, like a water nymph of unbelievable perfection, she rose out of the water and came steadily towards him. A surge of some primal instinct bathed him as he enclosed her in his robe. She must feel his body heat, as he could feel hers, but his only thought as he drew the folds of cloth around her was to keep her safe.

'You were watching me,' she accused softly, trembling a little as she slowly relaxed.

'Did you think I would let you swim on your own in the darkness? What if something had gone wrong?'

'I'm a strong swimmer, Raffa.'

'Even strong swimmers get cramp.'

During this short conversation he felt her growing awareness of their naked bodies touching. Casey's damp, his dry. And though he had ensured there was some fabric between them, it was hardly a barrier. He held her in his arms until she felt safe enough to rest her head against his chest. Savouring that for a moment, he shifted position, forcing Casey to move.

'Come on,' he said holding out his hand. 'We're both hungry.'

In a moment of complete trust she put her hand in his. 'I'm ready, Raffa.'

Raising her slender fingers to his lips, he said, 'I know.'

'Thank you again,' she said in a way that told him she didn't want to let her fantasies run away with her. Her next words confirmed it: 'Hopefully this will be the last time you'll have to bail me out.'

'And if it's not, you shouldn't worry. You can take advantage of me all you like.' He kept his robe around her, so she was hidden from sight but not from his senses as they walked back to camp. He could detect the clean oxygenated water, and even the sand between her toes, he was so keenly tuned to her. She was trying hard not to read too much into what had happened, while he was exulting. He said nothing until they reached the tented pavilion, where he moved the entrance flap for her.

'The robes are in the chest,' he reminded her. 'Help yourself.'

After he let the tent flap drop he stood a moment, breathing deeply, wondering how he was going to hold back from going straight to Casey now and making love to her all night. Anticipation, he mused, smiling a little as he walked away. Never had he felt hunger like this before. But the erotic build-up would put Casey's senses in a state of the utmost awareness, allowing her to extract the ultimate from each and every sensation—which was what he wanted for her.

She held her breath as she listened to Raffa walking away. For a moment she had thought he would come back into the tent, but he was going to make her wait—either that or he didn't want her after all.

That had to be it, she reasoned, pulling back from her stupid vigil. What was she waiting for, exactly?

Lifting the lid of the clothes chest, she selected the plainest robe in the smallest size. It was still far too big for her, but at least it was simple and serviceable and wouldn't draw attention. She didn't want to look as if she was trying too hard.

Having arranged it to cover as much of herself as she could, she scraped her still damp hair back into a ponytail before walking outside.

Raffa was stoking the fire, having removed his *howlis*. 'You look good in that,' he commented, casting a lazy glance over her.

And you look even better, Casey thought as his earring glinted when the flames rose. In fact, he looked amazing. What did she think she doing in the velvet night with the ruler of this country, when it was more a case of when rather than if she would beg him to seduce her.

'Didn't you find any sandals to fit?'

Jolted reluctantly from her daydream, Casey was immediately self-conscious in the face of Raffa's blistering glamour. 'No, I...I didn't think—'

Springing up, he handed her the long stick he was using to adjust the tinder. 'Watch the fire for me for a minute—and for goodness' sake stand well back from the flames.'

'I'm not a—' Too late. Raffa was gone. She could hear him moving about in the tent.

He was back moments later, with a pair of simple thonged sandals. 'Put these on. You'll feel better with something protecting your feet from the sand. The way it moves can make your feet ache after a while…'

And was there a cure for a heart that ached all the time? Casey wondered as she slipped her feet into the sandals.

They ate together seated on cushions outside the tent. From there, as Raffa had promised, they could see the stars. The simple meal Casey had suggested hadn't taken much preparation, but it had been long enough for their mood to return to the easy companionship they had established before the erotically charged episode at the oasis.

'This is good,' Raffa commented with approval as he wolfed down the last of the griddled halloumi cheese Casey had arranged in slices, alternated with fresh mango. She'd put a sprinkling of toasted pine nuts on top of the salad she had prepared. 'Where did you learn to cook like this?'

This definitely wasn't the moment to admit she had downloaded the recipe from a supermarket site. She had to keep her fantasy alive beneath the stars. 'I must have a natural talent.'

Raffa stopped chewing for a moment to stare at her. 'Either that or you used a recipe.'

They both laughed, and then he said, 'And as the next course is down to me I'll have to look to my laurels, I can see…'

So the unreconstructed alpha male could prepare food as well as look hotter than hell in a desert robe? Life just wasn't fair sometimes, Casey thought ruefully as Raffa sprang up.

'Figs,' he said, dangling them in front of her. 'Ripe, succulent, fresh from the tree.'

He made figs sound like the most erotic fruit on earth. She gulped as he selected a fat purple fruit just for her, and was so flustered by the time he touched it to her lips she managed to knock the coffee over.

'*Kab al gahwa khay!*' Raffa exclaimed.

'What did you say?'

'It's a good omen,' he explained. 'Knocking coffee over is

considered to be lucky in A'Qaban. So what I said to you was, bad luck often brings good luck in its wake.'

'Oh…'

Fat chance.

But the fig was delicious, and as she sucked the ripe pulp from the skin she tried not to notice how very thoroughly Raffa was doing the same.

'That was a good meal,' he said, having rinsed his hands in a bowl of water. Drying them on a soft towel, he held her gaze. 'I might keep you on as a chef if you're a good girl.'

'And if I'm bad you'll keep me twice as long?' She only meant it as a joke, but Raffa's eyes warned her not to play with fire.

He was just too much of a distraction in his black robes sitting next to her, but their night-time picnic beneath the stars had taken her back to being a child at camp, which she had enjoyed, and that safety blanket allowed her to relax. Leaning back on her hands, she gazed at the sky and it took her a moment to realise that Raffa had got up and was walking away.

'Where are you going?' She regretted the note of concern in her voice, because it made Raffa smile in a way that just wasn't safe.

'Would you rather I stayed?' he murmured

'No. No, of course not—I realise you must have lots to do.'

'Good. Then I'll leave you in the capable hands of these ladies.'

Casey turned to see a group of women hovering on the fringes of the trees. They were carrying earthenware jars, fluffy towels, and steaming jugs of fragranced water. 'What do they want?' Her voice was full of anxiety, to which Raffa responded with a careless gesture. 'Oh, to prepare you for the Sheikh, I expect.'

'*What?*' Casey whirled around to stare at the women, and by the time she turned back again Raffa had disappeared.

CHAPTER FOURTEEN

SHE could deal with most things, but this was way out of her comfort zone. She sprang to her feet as the women approached. 'No—no, thank you,' she said, fending them off with dramatic gestures. Every part of her that had been trembling with desire while Raffa was about had instantly shrivelled to a dried-up walnut. 'There must be some mistake,' she insisted when they kept on coming.

'No mistake,' one of the younger women explained in a cheerful voice with barely the trace of an accent. 'His Majesty thought you would enjoy a spa treatment after your long day. Please don't be alarmed, Ms Michaels. We anticipate many tourists will be coming to the desert to experience the special treatments passed down from generation to generation in A'Qaban. His Majesty told us that you will be responsible for encouraging this new industry, which is the reason he would like you to sample the various balms we have prepared.'

Ah.

'I see.' And she did see—unfortunately. Every time she thought her confidence was going to be rewarded by her fantasies becoming reality, Raffa turned things back to business. 'You speak perfect English.'

'I learned at the beauty college, where I trained...'

'Of course.' Casey blushed. 'Forgive me.'

'There is nothing to forgive,' the young girl said frankly with a friendly smile. 'I can well understand your surprise, finding beauticians waiting to trial their treatments on you in the middle of the desert. So, will you take the treatment, Ms Michaels?'

'I'd love to.' With her business head firmly in place, Casey told herself there was nothing to compare with first-hand experience.

There was a bath beneath the stars on a wooden platform, which the women filled with the warm, fragranced water before scattering its steaming surface with petals. They even arranged the greenery to make sure she would be completely private:

'That's the benefit of the oasis,' the young therapist explained. 'There's no shortage of screening here, and every product we use is fresh.'

'And wonderful,' Casey agreed, stepping into the water whilst the other woman held a towel to preserve her modesty. 'Oh, this is magic,' she murmured, sinking low and inhaling deeply, closing her eyes as she breathed in the delightful aroma of the water. 'What did you say it was? Only I'm tingling all over.'

'The rich scent of black coffee.'

'Raffa!' Water bounced over the side of the bath as Casey shot out of it. Realising he only had a towel wrapped around his waist and she was completely naked, she splashed down again, sinking as low as she could go.

'Combined with the earthy notes of native grass, temple incense and tree bark to lend a little warmth and woodiness,' he continued. 'Oh, and a touch of desert magic…'

'Where has everyone gone?' Casey demanded anxiously, looking around.

'That desert magic I mentioned.'

'Raffa—stop teasing me.' She crossed her arms over her chest. 'You've frightened the women away.'

'They bowed and left when I arrived.'

As they would to their king, she realised, trying to get her head around everything that was happening. Raffa's expression, however, was anything but regal. 'Arrogant—'

'Brute?' he suggested, his lips tugging with amusement as he moved closer to the platform on which her bath was resting. 'Well, what do you think of it?' he said, gesturing around. 'Do you think the intrepid explorers you hope to attract to A'Qaban will approve of a desert spa?'

'How could they not?' What did she think? *What did she think?* There wasn't a thought in her head that wasn't X-rated. Hard-muscled, toned and tanned, with just the right amount of chest hair, Raffa had a tattoo running from just below his neck to somewhere she wasn't prepared to look. If she had thought him sexy before, the ruler of A'Qaban half naked, with a rampant lion clambering all over him, was sin made flesh.

'You can come up now,' Raffa suggested. 'I've seen it all before—or had you forgotten?'

No, she hadn't forgotten, Casey thought, feeling deflated. The magic of the desert didn't seem to be working in her favour, somehow. 'So is this the end of my spa treatment?' She was feeling thoroughly fed up as Raffa picked up a towel.

'Not unless you want it to be…'

As he held it out, she demanded hoarsely, 'Raffa, is this fair?' And when he didn't respond, she insisted, 'Raffa, say something.'

'Adam al-Jawab jawab…'

'Say something I can understand.'

'Stand up first, and then I'll translate.' He jutted his chin when she hesitated. 'You don't want to catch cold, do you?'

Catch cold? She had enough heat for both of them. 'You promised to explain,' she insisted, as Raffa wrapped her warmly in a towel.

'No answer is an answer—or, as you might say, silence speaks volumes.'

'Well, that's no good if I can't understand your brand of silence,' Casey pointed out. Her first thought was to keep the conversation going, distracting Raffa from her extremely aroused nakedness beneath the towel, but then the penny dropped. 'Are you saying your being naked is fair?'

'You're naked, aren't you?'

'I'm here for a spa treatment.'

'So am I. And you're going to give it to me.'

Had the pussy cat found her claws? For a moment, as Casey gasped and looked truly alarmed, he wondered if she was ready for this. But then she gazed at him, and both challenge and determination crept into her eyes, and he changed his mind. He preferred a match of equals, but women constantly disappointed him. Casey was proving to be the exception to that. Money and status, in particular, were the last things on her mind.

Casey was searching for reality, one she could deal with. He wanted her to know a reality that existed beyond the pages of her parents' books. That was one of the reasons he had brought her here. It was his intention to prove that there was nothing to be ashamed of in the naked body, that in all its exciting variations it was beautiful; he intended to start this tutorial with his own.

'Come,' he said, holding out his hand to her. He walked unselfconsciously, aware that Casey was trying very hard not to look at him.

He walked with her from the open-air bathroom into the main part of the tent where, at his instruction, the women had left the creams and oils she would need to perform the treatment he had in mind.

'I'll just climb up on the bed,' he said, dropping his towel.

'The bed?' she gasped.

'We'll call it the treatment couch, if you prefer.'

'I do prefer,' she assured him, staring fixedly away.

He hid his smile to save her blushes. That he should meet a woman so fresh and challenging had really opened his eyes. He could share his life with a woman like this—a woman who could fulfil public duties at his side with the same enthusiasm that she should for other, more caring issues, closer to his heart. But he was wedded to duty and to A'Qaban, he reminded himself sternly. There had never been any room in his life for the self-indulgence of a love affair.

'Well? Get up on the couch,' Casey rapped impatiently, bringing his honourable thoughts to an abrupt close.

She plunged her arms up to the elbows in a tub of cream. She could do this. She *would* do this. Timid virgin or not, she had confidence. She just needed to dig deep and prove it—to herself and to Raffa. To herself mostly, Casey admitted silently.

'Don't forget to warm your hands up first,' Raffa told her dryly, moving his face to one side as he eased his position on the couch.

'Don't worry—I will.' They were warm already—very warm—and so was she.

She hadn't looked at Raffa properly yet. She needed a moment to prepare before doing that. She glanced at his towel on the floor, and checked her own towel was securely fastened.

Casey's breath caught in her throat as she took her first look at Raffa's naked form

'Steady,' he warned as she slapped two handfuls of goo on his back. 'Half of that landed on the floor.'

Possibly because she had her eyes tightly shut. 'I read somewhere that a firm touch is needed,' she defended, wondering if the spasms of delight she was experiencing would ever stop racing from her fingertips to her arms, from where they spread outwards to every part of her body.

'Firm, but not slapdash,' Raffa agreed huskily. 'Would you like me to show you how?'

Rippling with muscle, there wasn't an ounce of fat on him anywhere— which was quite a bit different from her own well-upholstered form. 'No, that's all right—I'm sure I'll get the hang of it.'

'Rub the cream in well, but catch any dribbles on the towel first.'

'Dribbles?'

'Of cream?'

'On my towel?'

'On any towel…'

Leaning over him, she managed to hold onto the towel with her elbow and dab at him with the hem at the same time.

'Don't be so prissy—rub it in.'

Casey stared at Raffa's sculpted shoulders before tentatively resting her fingertips against them.

'Now, rub.'

Her whole body fired in response to the warm, firm flesh beneath her hands.

'Use more pressure…'

She leaned against the couch, craving contact with Raffa in places that had never felt this much action before.

'More…'

More? How could there be more than this? She felt swollen in certain places, short of breath, and hungry for Raffa in a way that made her throat tight and everything else rather too loose.

'More pressure, Casey…'

'I'm using all I can.'

'Pathetic,' he growled. 'Try harder.'

Any harder than this and she'd explode. But she had to try, Casey told herself firmly. She couldn't back down now. She explored the wide expanse of Raffa's back with infinite care and absolute slowness. If she was going to do this, she was going to enjoy every minute of it. Closing her eyes, she used a little more pressure, and was rewarded by Raffa's sigh.

'Nice?' she murmured.

'Don't distract yourself by talking—I'll tell you when to stop.'

'Okay…' But he felt so good, so warm and full of energy; she wanted to be a lot closer to him than this. She leaned over, pressing herself against Raffa's side, longing to ease the pressure inside her.

'That's much better,' he said, with the suggestion of a smile in his voice. 'I think you're getting the hang of it at last…'

His face was deadpan, and his deep voice was muffled

against his powerful forearms as she worked on his back, but his sigh of pleasure gave him away—he was enjoying this as much as she was. She took a detour over his bulging biceps and on down each of his forearms, which gave her the opportunity to press her chest against his back…

'Much, much better,' he husked contentedly.

She was enjoying herself so much by this time she wasn't prepared when he turned on his back. 'Now feel me,' he said.

'Feel you?' She gulped.

'My chest… Feel it… Explore, Casey.'

She shut her eyes and started tentatively to do as Raffa had suggested. But as she explored she grew bolder. He was magnificent. Raffa was a magnificent fighting machine…or a lover.

'And don't forget there's more to me than my chest…'

She was already incredibly aware of that. Luckily her towel was still in place to hide her arousal, though the friction of it against her painfully erect nipples was almost unbearable.

She had to brazen it out. She had to be brave enough to bear the pleasure-pain of pure arousal and distract herself by tracing the hard band of muscle above Raffa's waist.

Could anything be more delicious that that? It was too soon to find out, and so she turned her attention to his feet. She'd work her way up. Well, part-way up. Two could play at Raffa's game. He was not just acquainting her with his body, he was teasing her—and enjoying it.

He had extremely sexy feet. Moving on from there, she tested rock-hard calves, before moving on to the firmest thighs she had ever seen. Not that she had seen many, of course…

'That's enough,' Raffa said, sitting up.

'How did I do?'

'Better than I imagined,' he told her dryly. Swooping down, he picked up his towel. 'And now it's your turn.'

'But…'

'No buts—other than the naked kind. Climb up.'

'On the bed?'

'That's the general idea—though don't you prefer to call it a treatment couch?' His voice was mocking.

She was supposed to climb up and lie naked on a treatment couch still warm from Raffa's own naked body?

That's the one, Casey told her timid self, clutching her towel tightly around her.

'Without the towel?'

'Without. How am I supposed to give you a massage if you're wearing a towel?'

'Er...'

'Exactly. So, please lose it.'

Closing her eyes tightly, as if that meant Raffa couldn't see her either, she chucked the towel on the rug beneath the treatment couch and scrambled up. Clinging onto it for dear life, she tried to ignore the seductive warmth already seeping through her veins and the violent heat painting her cheeks bright red.

'Are you comfortable?' Raffa asked.

With him staring at her naked body...?

'Relax.'

'I might be able to if you'd stop reading my mind.'

'I'm reading your muscles—they're all bunched up...'

The touch of Raffa's hands was indescribable. He had a wonderful natural skill that banished all signs of tension within the first few seconds. Her only complaint now was that by confining his attentions to her back he perversely made her think very rude thoughts indeed.

She wanted a lot more than Raffa was prepared to give, Casey realised—this really was just a massage.

'Is the pressure okay for you?'

As Raffa kneaded her all too compliant shoulders, she managed, 'Perfect...' Perfect for her shoulders, that was, but she wanted him to touch her intimately.

Sighing, she closed her eyes, wondering how to transmit that feeling. Should she purse her lips like this? Or loosen her mouth

just a little and stare at Raffa with her own particular brand of
sultry? Should she try a little moue and then look away? Or just
brazen it out? Maybe she should tease and run—

'Have you done with all available facial expressions, or
would you like to try for one more?'

She came to with a jolt, noticing that at sometime Raffa had
pulled on his robe. 'Is my treatment over?' Must she sound quite
so disappointed?

'For now.'

For now? The real question was *what next?*

What came next was the biggest surprise of all. It seemed
Raffa had no difficulty communicating his feelings, and he
would quite like to kiss her too, she saw when he smiled faintly
as he held her gaze.

'How do you do that?'

'Read your thoughts?' As he spoke he lifted her into a seated
position on the bed in front of him and brought his face within
kissable distance of hers. 'Years of dedicated practice…'

Casey frowned. Did she want to know that?

She could always join Raffa's class, her bolder self suggested.

Join his class and then insist on private lessons, Casey concluded optimistically. 'You're obviously way ahead of me in
that—so perhaps I need more tuition.'

'I'm sure you do,' Raffa agreed. 'Could you face another ride?'

A ride? 'How will that help?' She covered herself with the
towel. Raffa might have no inhibitions, but it wasn't catching.

'I want to show you something. Are you up for it?'

'What is it?'

'A place I'd like to show you.'

'Somewhere special?'

'Somewhere that means a lot to me.'

'Your palace?'

'Come on—you can take a cushion with you.' As he spoke
he chucked her a cushion and she caught it.

'What's this for?'

'For the horse,' he said. 'To protect his back from you bouncing up and down on it.'

Laughing, she chucked the cushion back at him, and somehow in between the tension between them disappeared.

'Or,' Raffa said as he thought about it, 'you could ride in front of me. We'll travel faster that way.'

'Do I have to ride at all?'

His eyes darkened with amusement. 'The more you ride, the easier it gets.'

'Do I really look that gullible?' Casey demanded, smiling at him as she planted her hands on her hips.

'Shall we find out?' Raffa challenged. 'Come on.' In his hands there was a shimmer of something blue. 'Get dressed and we'll go.'

'What is this?' Casey held up the exquisite silver-embroidered robe Raffa handed her. 'This isn't the robe I was wearing earlier.'

'But you've been prepared for the Sheikh since then.'

'Hah!' Casey exclaimed, balling it up and tossing it back at him. 'I'll wear trousers for riding, thank you. And I should remind you—'

'What?' Raffa cut across her with a very wicked look indeed.

'I'm pretty hopeless on a horse.'

'But I'm not,' he pointed out. 'So no excuses.'

She had never felt safer or more at risk in her life. Seated in front of Raffa on his magnificent black stallion, it was impossible to feel she might tumble to the ground—but that was no help when it came to the far worse peril of falling in love.

The sensation of having her long hair streaming behind her as the stallion raced across the desert plain while Raffa held her safe was amazing. If he had decided to think up the most romantic journey on earth, he couldn't have made a better job of it. The sky was littered with stars, while the moon lit their way, and the mountains were jagged fingers that seemed to beckon her ever deeper into the wild land that Raffa called home. He held the reins loosely in one hand and kept her close with the other. She could feel his warmth and his strength, could hear his heart beating, while his fresh minty breath brushed her cheek.

Closing her eyes, she leaned back, allowing her hips to move to the rhythm of the stallion's explosive gait. Far from hating horse-riding, as she always had, she was beginning to love it, and to hope the magical journey could last for ever.

It would last for ever in her memory, at least. How could it not, when she was riding through the desert night in front of a sheikh who encapsulated every fantasy hero she'd ever had? With his black robes flying behind him and his face hidden behind the mysterious *howlis*. She was wrapped in an erotic fantasy that far exceeded everything she could dream up.

And Raffa's palace? Casey wondered. What would that be like?

It would be located far from the public gaze, she decided, and protected by the granite peaks they were riding towards. It would be hard to find—it would be an eyrie, a fortress, a lair fit for the golden lion of the desert. There would be sumptuous rooms protected from the relentless desert sun beneath cupolas of solid gold, and there would be intimate courtyards where lovers could meet unobserved. On the walls inside the palace there would be painted erotic scenes, and of course a sheikh-sized bed, over which a softly whirring fan would turn lazily to cool the lovers on their tangled sheets. Jewel-studded walls would bear silent witness to their lovemaking, while fountains in the garden beyond the windows would sing a siren song to the rhythm of their sighs...

CHAPTER FIFTEEN

As HE reined in, slowing the pace to allow the stallion to pick his way along the rocky approach to the mountains, he wondered what Casey was thinking. She had been quiet for a while now, and she was such a dreamer. He hoped she wouldn't be too disappointed by what he had to show her. He was opening up part of his life to Casey, because the hunt for someone to work for him had become so much more, and he was hungry to find out everything there was to know about Casey Michaels.

Urging his stallion *Raad*—the word meant thunder in A'Qabani—up the first incline, he noticed the great stallion's ears prick up as he scented the place they both loved—the place they both considered home.

For once Casey was lost for words.

Raffa turned to her. 'You're not disappointed?'

She looked at him as he brought the prancing stallion to a restless halt.

'Disappointed? How could I be?' They were at the foot of a sheer cliff, where an icy stream, its source hidden somewhere far above them, tumbled in a series of frothing waterfalls to a moonlit pool. This had to be one of the lesser known wonders of the world.

Springing down from the saddle, Raffa reached up to help

her dismount. 'You'll find the water surprisingly warm—
though I should warn you the torrent coming down from the
peaks is freezing cold.'

'But the pool is heated by the sun?'

'The relentless desert sun,' Raffa agreed, holding her just
above the ground so their faces were disturbingly level.

'You can put me down now…please?'

His eyes beneath the concealing *howlis* glinted dangerously.
'Or I could throw you in.'

'Please…please don't.' With humour…His eyes were
glinting with humour, Casey saw with relief. 'So you've
brought me to another spa?'

'Nature's spa,' Raffa agreed.

She could have happily stayed in his arms for ever, but the
horse was stamping impatiently and so she stepped away,
while Raffa slipped the reins over his stallion's head.
Unfastening the girth, he removed the saddle. She took it from
him and rested it carefully against the stubbly trunk of a palm
tree while Raffa led the stallion round to let him cool down.
When it was safe for him to drink, Raffa removed the bridle
too and set him loose.

Casey's heart ached with longing. She wanted so much more
than Raffa was prepared to give. She watched him stroke the
stallion's quivering flanks, knowing what she would do for that
same soothing touch. Raffa was so good at everything—he had
even made her forget her own lack of skill on horseback, to the
point where she'd almost believed she could ride.

Ride? She could fly with Raffa's arms around her.

But she mustn't make too much out of this expedition. If
anything had been going to happen between them it would have
happened at the oasis. This was just an opportunity for Raffa to
share the treasures of his country with her; treasures she would
be expected to market to the world if she got the job…

'Come on,' he said, stretching out his hand to her.

'Come where?' She hung back, suddenly feeling shy and uncertain now the horse was happily drinking and Raffa's attention was all on her.

'I want you to see something. You have a little climb ahead of you.'

'A *little* climb?' Casey glanced anxiously at the sheer rock wall in front of her.

'I can carry you, if you like.'

Hearing the amusement in his voice, she assured him, 'I'm quite capable of standing on my own two feet, thank you.'

'There is a path, but it isn't the one you're taking,' he said, catching up with her in a couple of strides.

'Oh…' She stared about.

'It's not obvious unless you know where to look.'

'And you, of course, know where to look?'

'I like to think so…' Raffa's dangerous black gaze held hers.

'Then you'd better show me where to go.'

But he didn't move.

She took a deep steadying breath. It wasn't easy, containing all the emotion inside her, and as Raffa continued to stare down at her she felt as if this was a pivotal moment in her emotional journey—in her life. Raffa had given her the confidence to admit she wanted him, but did Raffa want *her?*

A breeze ruffled the scrub around them, but when she whispered his name he remained silent. 'Raffa, please,' she repeated, 'can I ask you something?'

He knew the moment had arrived. Casey's fantasy world had finally collided with the real world, and he wasn't in the least surprised when all her pent-up frustrations poured out.

'Raffa, what would you say if I asked you to make love to me?'

'I would tell you that you're a virgin and that you should be very sure.' He could see Casey thinking. Was the fact that she was a virgin branded on her forehead?

'How can you tell?'

'Years of experience?' he suggested with a faint smile.

'Please don't tease me, Raffa—not now.'

He started to unwind his *howlis*. This was what he'd wanted since he had first set eyes on Casey, but was reality the last thing on her mind? He had enjoyed watching Casey grow in confidence, to the point where she trusted him even when she was naked, but was he just her fantasy? He decided to postpone his verdict for now.

'Shall I lead the way?' he suggested, glancing up the path.

She nodded her head, desperately trying to hide her disappointment.

Casey had a lot to learn—not least was that anticipation increased the pleasure of the final outcome. She had made him think that was no longer in doubt now.

They were halfway up the first slope when they turned a corner and a natural platform in the rock was revealed. Broad and sheltered from the elements, as well as from the waterfall that fell by the side of it, it had been worn smooth by the pressure of many feet over the years.

'I thought we'd set up camp here.'

'For the night?' Casey couldn't help sounding worried.

'You're hungry, aren't you?'

'Hungry? Yes.' Now she couldn't help sounding relieved. She had just one more concern. 'Where's the bathroom?'

'Choose your bush. And your warm bath's down the slope, with a nice icy shower to follow.'

'I think I'll start by making a fire.'

'You?' Raffa was on his way down the slope to collect some more things and he stopped.

'Why not me?' She might be useless at the game of love, but she could start a fire, and she pulled a firestone out of her pocket to prove it.

Raffa laughed—a flash of strong white teeth to relieve the tension she was almost as good at building as a fire. 'I had forgotten your firestone,' he admitted.

She watched him all the way down as far as she could. Raffa

moved with the agility of a mountain lion—the same lion that was the symbol of dauntless courage, bravery and valour. When he was out of sight she cupped her hands to nurture the tiny flame she'd managed to kindle from the available tinder. She was usually better than this at setting a fire, but while her mind was on the job in hand her heart was still with Raffa.

This was a complete and utter indulgence. He couldn't remember how long it had been since he had taken a break like this in his favourite part of the desert. Years ago, when he'd been on breaks from the army, he had come here all the time, and it refreshed him and made sense of things…

Made sense of things except for Casey, he amended; the desert had failed him where she was concerned. He stared back up the cliff face, to where a plume of smoke signified success. He smiled. She was never short of a surprise, and he enjoyed her company, but life was never that simple. The only thing he could be sure of was that she'd got the job. The details might be a little hazy right now, but Casey wouldn't be leaving A'Qaban any time soon.

He returned with rugs, food and drink and other supplies, to find Casey on her hands and knees, blowing determinedly at the one branch that had refused to light. 'Are you sure you don't need any help there?' He came to hunker down beside her, re-sisting the temptation to touch her.

'Well, now you come to mention it.' She turned to look at him. 'I could use some help with my hand.'

'Your hand?'

'Yes. It seems to be shaking…'

They came together like a force of nature. It was impossible to know who moved first. Her nipples rose, her breath quick-ened, and she was instantly and completely aroused as Raffa claimed her mouth with a fierce and possessive hunger.

The tension between them could never have held. The instant Raffa's hand covered Casey's she gladly threw away every semblance of self-control. But there was more. Pleasure hit so fast she gave a wail of astonishment as she tumbled headlong into a violent climax. Raffa held her safe in his arms as she moaned, 'Oh, no. Oh, no…' But the pleasure waves just kept on coming. He kissed her brow, her eyelids and her mouth, until finally she quietened into an embarrassed silence and pulled away from him.

Burying her head in her hands, she wished herself a million miles away.

'Casey?' Raffa murmured gently. Cupping her face in his hands, he stared into her eyes. 'This isn't right for you.'

'Who decides that?' she demanded in a small voice. 'You?'

He remained silent. This was his fault. He had allowed things to move too fast. He had wanted to share this special place with Casey, but he had underestimated her feelings for him. He shouldn't have allowed his desire for her to show; she was too young, too innocent. 'I should never have brought you here—'

'Yes, you should,' she argued passionately. 'I should know the country I'm supposed to be selling to the world.'

'Casey, Casey…' Taking hold of her wrists, he drew her hands away from her face with the utmost care. 'I think we both know this has gone far beyond an interview for a job, and however much I might want to, I can never give you all the things you deserve.'

'I don't want anything from you,' she protested.

She never would want anything from him in the material sense, he knew that; but there were other things Casey deserved. 'You'd want my time, wouldn't you?'

The look in her eyes stabbed into his heart. 'Well, I can't give you time,' he said cruelly, to save her before she got into this any deeper. 'A'Qaban takes up all my time and you deserve better than that. If I make love to you things will change.'

'Why must they change?'

Only innocence could prompt that question, but as he

reached for her she turned away. 'Casey, I'm already married—
to duty and to my country.'

'Who mentioned marriage?' she flared, turning back to him.

He remained silent. He might not have known Casey for more
than a few days, but he knew her well enough to understand something of her hopes and dreams. An affair was not what she wanted,
and it would break her eventually. 'Forgive me?' he whispered.

'Forgive you?' She frowned in bewilderment.

'Please…' Taking her hands in his, he raised them to his lips.
All his life he had been the hunter, but now his only thought
was to protect Casey from further hurt.

'One last kiss?' she suggested hopefully.

He looked at the smile on her face. It might have worked if
her eyes hadn't been full of tears. 'Come here…' He put a shel-
tering arm around her. She was so warm and so vulnerable, and
he could only imagine how humiliating she must be finding this.

He dipped his head with the intention of kissing her once
more, chastely on the cheek. However painful that would be for
both of them, he meant it to be a goodbye to that side of things.

And he thought he knew her?

She ripped his *howlis* from his head with surprising force,
and, twining her fingers in his hair, she dragged him close.

'What do you think you're doing?' he demanded in surprise.

'I think you know,' she said steadily.

He could pull away at any time, but he wanted to make her
see sense first. 'Casey, don't be silly—' But he would never hurt
her and she held on.

One of his hands found its way to the hollow at the base of
her spine, where she felt so fragile. A sullen wind chose that
moment to whip their faces, and as concern overrode caution
he drew her beneath his robe so she could share his warmth.

In that moment he was lost. The erotic world he had been
resisting claimed him. The feel of Casey's body against his, the
thunder of her heart and the whisper of her breath—he was
kissing her, and not at all chastely.

As he kissed her, he reached for her hand, lacing their fingers together. It was a promise from him to keep her safe. It was a promise she understood, and when she looked at him with trust in her eyes their positions were reversed, and he was hers to do with as she liked.

They kissed and caressed in front of the dwindling fire in a way he hadn't done since adolescence, until—'Have I made you cry?' He frowned, tasting her tears.

'I blame you,' she said, laughing and crying softly at the same time.

'Explain,' he insisted. His lips were tugging with amusement as he brought her round to face him.

'Don't laugh at me, Raffa.' She touched his lips and he was instantly serious. 'No one has ever made me confront my fears before.'

'And you're still frightened?'

'Yes,' she admitted.

'You have always thought lovemaking must be rough, painful and fast, with all the pleasure on the man's side?' he suggested.

She couldn't believe she was talking about something like this with Raffa. This was something she hadn't even been able to discuss with her own parents—and they were experts in the field.

'You think a man must take absolute control and you are expected to lie beneath him and endure whatever happens as best you can?'

'How do you know that?' Then she smiled, remembering how Raffa had teased her. 'Years of experience?' she said, pretending disapproval, but then she laughed, and they both clung to that shred of humour.

'Did you think I was going to throw you over my shoulder and carry you off to the desert as my captive virgin?' Raffa suggested. Thumbing his jaw, he added thoughtfully, 'That's not a bad idea, actually…'

'Raffa,' she scolded, by now completely relaxed.

'Maybe you would have preferred that?' he said, holding her

in a loose embrace in front of him. 'And there's still time,' he warned, pretending to be fierce.

'But I trust you,' she said.

'I should hope so.'

'I still have hang-ups.'

'Only because you don't know the rules.'

'What rules?'

'Rule number one: no hang-ups allowed in the desert.'

If only it were that simple, Casey thought, hugging herself. She had just made a spectacle of herself in front of Raffa in the most acutely embarrassing way. He had talked her round and reassured her, but she was still aroused. She had never been so aroused. Her nipples were on fire and she was throbbing with need between her legs, where she felt swollen and moist. She had never wanted sex more and never been more certain that she wouldn't know what to do if they made love—except that she would make a complete and utter hash of it.

'Dreaming again. Or just worrying?' Raffa prompted.

'I'd be useless at it,' she blurted out.

'Useless at what?'

'Sex.'

He made a low, confident masculine sound. 'But I'm not...' Touching her chin, he made her look at him.

'This isn't funny, Raffa.'

'No, it isn't,' he agreed, turning serious. 'You have parents who advise other people with sexual problems, and for some reason you seem to think you have all those same problems yourself.'

'I *know* I have,' she interrupted.

'How do you know?'

'I can get so far down the road and then I can't go any further. I've read the books, so I know—'

'You don't know anything,' he interrupted. 'How can you know anything when you're still a virgin? You've read too many books, Casey, and life has to be experienced outside of

the covers of a book. Books are instructive and interesting—
and surprising, sometimes—but they can never take the place
of living in the moment and all that that entails: feeling, sharing,
caring, cherishing, laughing, crying.'

'Loving?' She stared at him steadily until she read the
answer in his eyes.

'Loving in the moment? Yes, of course.'

That was Casey's cue to move away from him. He knew it
was a lousy answer, but he had nothing to offer her long-term,
and he wouldn't pretend. Casey was special—very special. But
she made him feel like the worst type of man as she hugged her
knees, burying her face again. It was as if all the good that had
been done over the past few days had been wasted.

'I'm sorry.'

'No—I'm sorry.' She cut across him, lifting her head. There
were no tears now, just an expression of resignation, which he
found almost worse. 'I shouldn't have pressed you like this. I've
got no right.' She threw her hands up in mock despair. 'I don't
know what I was thinking.'

Everything she was entitled to think—that he had brought
her here to make love to her. It was a perfectly reasonable sup-
position. He just wished Casey didn't believe her parents' books
held the answer to everything, or that fairytales could sometimes come true.

Picking up the *howlis* from his neck, he readjusted it until only
his eyes were showing. 'I'm not a very romantic Sheikh, am I?'

'Oh, I don't know…' She stared with him into the vastness
of the desert. 'You brought me here.'

The wry tone in her voice was so much better to hear than
Casey's awkwardness and uncertainty. 'Should I try harder?'
he suggested dryly.

'You can try…'

'Your eyes are like stars,' he intoned solemnly. 'Will that do?'

'I suppose it will have to.'

She was still smiling when a cloud scudded across the moon,

plunging them into darkness. Sensing her unease, he reached for her. 'Don't tell me you're frightened of the dark as well?'

When the cloud rolled away she was staring up at him. As he met her gaze he wondered if this was the most intimate moment he had ever shared with anyone. And then she whispered, 'Make love to me, Raffa…'

CHAPTER SIXTEEN

WITHIN moment Casey's mind was wiped clear of why she shouldn't, or mustn't, and above all why she couldn't. Every excuse her lack of self-confidence had ever thrown at her was effectively obliterated by Raffa's overwhelming sensuality. She had never felt passion like this before and pressed close, her breasts aching for his touch.

When he deepened the kiss, plundering her mouth in a brazen imitation of what he'd like to do to her, swollen lips pulsed with need and she groaned her approval. 'Oh, please,' she begged, clinging fiercely to him. 'Don't you dare change your mind now.'

There was no chance of that.

Raffa removed her clothes with ease.

The words 'years of experience' flashed between them in a look. The revelation that sex could be fun boosted Casey's confidence. It had always looked like such a serious undertaking between the covers of her parents' books. But with Raffa—

That was as much thought as she could manage before Raffa's lips crushed her mouth, opening her lips with the pressure of his, invading and tasting her, only to pull back and tease her with his tongue, tracing the line of her mouth, before plunging deep again, in a blatant rehearsal of what he meant to do to her.

She was on fire for him, every part of her pleading for his touch, for his attention. Mindless with delight, she bucked towards him. A dam had broken, and now her hunger was released she wanted everything he could give her.

She offered her breasts, begging in words she hardly recognised for him to ease the ache inside her. Taking her nipples, he chafed them while soothing her with words in A'Qabani. But she refused to be soothed. Her nipples were almost painfully extended, and the pleasure was streaming between her legs, where it gathered in insistent pulses.

Raffa's answer was to brush her nipples with his lips, and then he suckled while his hands explored, tracing a leisurely path over her quivering belly towards the source of her need.

She was almost frantic with desire by this time. She had waited so long for this moment, and was almost frightened of losing control again before Raffa could complete his investigations.

'Are you warm enough?' he demanded, when she shuddered uncontrollably.

Desire swirled around her, making it impossible to answer. She could only thrash beneath him, seeking more contact. These feelings, these incredible sensations—all of them new, and all of them so much stronger and more intense than she had dreamed.

'There's only one way to be sure,' Raffa growled. 'I'll have to cover you all over.'

She gasped as he swung her beneath him, and then rubbed herself shamelessly against him, catching what pressure she could from his powerful thigh. 'Please…' she managed shakily, hungry for more pleasure.

'You want more…?'

'Everything,' she groaned, opening herself to him.

Raffa tugged his robe over his head. He was naked underneath. He was magnificent…

'I always wondered what a Sheikh wore underneath his robes,' she murmured, reaching up to trace his ferocious tattoo.

'Well, now you know.'

'A condom *and* a tattoo.'

'It's enough, don't you think?'

'More than—' Casey's words were choked off as Raffa's hand found its place between her legs with unerring accuracy.

'Good?' he murmured, testing her readiness.

She could only writhe with greedy delight. There could be nothing better than this, surely? Closing her eyes, she gave herself up to pleasure as Raffa worked with the greatest skill and sensitivity, until she was so engorged with need she could only whimper, 'I need you…I need you…please…please…' But though he teased and stimulated, he refused her release. 'Oh, please don't stop.' She was practically sobbing with disappointment when he changed position.

'Who says I'm stopping? I want you to feel me…'

Casey's mouth dried. Reaching down nervously, she gasped at the size of him, but even as she shrank away Raffa moved so he could touch her with just the tip of his erection. 'I would never hurt you, Casey.'

'Oh…' Her mouth fell loose. This was more sensation than she had ever known. Her breathing changed, quickened, as if every part of her was waiting, but he was so big, so huge…

Raffa was kissing her, deeply and persuasively, until all her fears dissolved and she was crushing her mouth against his, hungry for more contact, more pressure, more pleasure—more of everything he had to give her…

She was so tender and vulnerable beneath him, and yet she was driven by a hunger equal to his own. She had taken his shoulders in a vice-like grip and was urging him on with words that surprised him.

'Okay, we can do that,' he murmured, grinning against her mouth. This was all he had ever wanted for Casey…all he had ever wanted.

Her eyes had turned almost black, with just a slim ring of cobalt surrounding the dilated pupil. His must be the same. He wanted her as he had never wanted any woman before, and he eased her thighs a little wider. He found her to be just as he'd expected only better—plump, warm and moist, and oh, so eager. He teased her with the tip again, for the sheer pleasure of hearing her soft cry of delight.

'Please, Raffa…Please…'

'Patience,' he murmured against her lips, moving rhythmically so that each time he caught a little deeper inside her.

'No—now,' she insisted fiercely, taking the decision out of his hands by bucking towards him. 'Oh, Raffa,' she moaned, as he moved with infinite steadiness to claim her completely.

However much he wanted this he would never allow himself to forget how inexperienced she was. 'Am I hurting you?'

'If you stop now I'll never ever forgive you…'

For ever was a long, long time he thought—and then, inevitably, the world outside real time slipped away.

Her world was composed of Raffa. Her concentration was all on him—on his muscular back beneath her fingers, and his rock-hard chest in front of her face, and the sublime rocking motion that was taking her places she had always wanted to go. Her eyes were full of him, and her ears were tuned to his erotic suggestions in A'Qabani. Her world was pleasure—pleasure that defied belief as Raffa settled deep inside her. He inhabited her completely—and not just her body, but her mind, her soul, her heart.

He stretched her beyond anything she would have believed possible before this moment, and as she grew accustomed to the new sensation of being one he withdrew. There was barely chance to voice her complaint before he plunged deep again, to her shriek of surprised delight.

'For the pleasure of taking you again,' he murmured against her smile. 'And again.'

He moved faster now, in firm, measured strokes, but the build was so great the destination began to terrify her. 'I can't—'

'Yes, you can,' Raffa insisted. 'I'll keep you safe.'

'No…. Please…Really…I can't—'

'Yes,' he told her firmly, continuing the steady onslaught on her senses.

Seconds later she was keening with surprise as ecstasy consumed her. As the violent pleasure took her over completely Raffa held her safe, as he said he'd would, and when she calmed he continued his steady rhythm until her throbbing flesh demanded more.

'I can't…not again,' she said more in wonder than surprise.

'But you want to?' Raffa smiled wickedly down at her.

'You know I do,' she gasped out, locking her legs around his waist.

'Then you can.' And, cupping her buttocks in his strong, firm hands, he proved it so.

'Is there a temptation to do nothing but this once you get the hang of it?' Casey demanded groggily some hours later. Snuggled safe in Raffa's arms, on their soft bed of rugs over-looking the desert, she was gazing out at a dawn-spangled sky. Lilac competed with tangerine clouds, and there were aqua smudges and lacy hairs of light along the horizon. It was a dis-traction, but not enough of one to keep her gaze from feasting on Raffa's naked form, currently entangled with her own.

'I think you'll find it's necessary to take one or two breaks,' he observed, winding a curl of her hair around his finger to draw her close.

'Well, I think that's absolutely outrageous,' Casey whispered against his lips. 'And quite unnecessary.'

'Do I take it you want more?' Raffa said this approvingly, drawing her on top of him as he spoke. 'Surely you don't want to miss the sunrise in the desert? It's the reason I brought you here…'

'Then you'll have to bring me here again…'

Making love with Raffa was the ultimate joy, the ultimate freedom.

Or the biggest self deluding screw-up yet?

No, Casey argued with her inner voice. She wouldn't let self-doubt spoil this moment. Raffa might be a king and married to his kingdom, but she'd take this for what it was and then walk away.

Oh, really…?

Clinging to him, she kissed him passionately, but the feeling that this was a dream, and the fantasy she indulged in back home was the only reality, refused to go away.

CHAPTER SEVENTEEN

'So…is your palace far from here?' Casey asked Raffa, remembering she had thought that was the point of this expedition.

'My palace?' Loose-limbed and sexier than ever in the aftermath of sex, he rolled onto his back to stare into the brightening sky. '*This* is my palace…'

'This…?' Joining him, Casey exclaimed softly when she saw what he was looking at. A pair of eagles was swooping and wheeling in what appeared to be an intricate courtship dance.

'Can you think of anything more beautiful?' Raffa murmured.

No, she couldn't Casey thought, watching the great birds swerve and dive.

Raffa sat up, completely unconcerned that he was naked. 'Shall we go for a swim?'

'Has the water warmed up yet?'

Wrapping a rug around her shoulders to keep her warm, he cupped her chin and dipped his head to drop a kiss on her lips.

Her eyes were closed, and she was suspended in that moment longer than he was, Casey realised, opening her eyes to find Raffa already slipping his robe over his head. Reaching for her clothes, she started to put them on. A sense of inevitability had gripped her, as if this marked the beginning of the end. She shook it off determinedly as Raffa turned to speak to her.

'Come as you are,' he said; 'that's all you need.'

As he reached for her hand, she took hold of it with confidence. He hoisted her to her feet and then paused by the cliff edge, staring out across the vast plain.

'Are you expecting someone?' she teased him. There wasn't a sign of human trespass other than theirs.

'The wilderness grounds me,' he said. 'It reminds me who I am and where I've come from.'

And where he must go back to? Casey wondered with a shiver of dread. 'Will you tell me about your parents?' she said, clinging on to what felt like their rapidly disappearing time together.

For a moment she thought she had gone too far, but then with a shrug Raffa lifted his powerful shoulder. 'What I can remember of them,' he said.

'If you don't want to—'

'No, I do…' He came away from the edge and stood in the shadow of the mountain. 'They were killed in a coup many years ago. I was just a baby at the time. My mother could have left the country and fled to safety with me. Instead she sent me to England with a relative, while she stayed on in A'Qaban with my father.'

'What a beautiful love story—and how tragic.'

'Yes, it was both of those things.'

As Raffa spoke, his voice so cool and distant, Casey's heart went out to him. 'They certainly gave you something to live up to.'

'Something to live for…' He spoke firmly, and there was a message in his words that made her fears that their time together was limited all the more real.

She reached for his hand. At first he was unresponsive, but then slowly his fingers relaxed and laced with hers. He'd made her think about the close-knit family she had left behind in England. She couldn't bear to think that all the good the desert had done Raffa had been undone because of her.

'I had a very lucky upbringing, and I didn't mean to pry—'

'Yes, you did.' The tug of the old humour on his lips was more than she could have hoped for. 'That's not unreasonable,' he went on. 'In your place I would have done exactly the same.'

'And now?' Lifting her hands, she let them drop to her sides, wondering why she had to blurt out everything in her head.

'Stop worrying,' Raffa said, reading her as easily as he always had. 'Now we swim.'

'Okay…' She made a pretence of smiling. This was as good as it seemed. She was having the adventure of a lifetime, and maybe it was the start of something even more than that…

Why shouldn't it be? Casey demanded, when smutty little doubt demons came to haunt her.

'What's this?' Casey ran excitedly from tree to tree when they reached the rock pool. She reached up to free a plump ripe peach from a palm tree. 'Did you do this?'

Raffa held out his arms and smiled. 'That's the trouble with you city girls.' He caught her to him when she returned with her prize. 'You've got no imagination. No,' he insisted when she brought the ripe fruit to her lips, 'you can't eat it before you've paid for it.'

'And how am I going to do that with no money to hand? You're impossible,' she exclaimed, seeing his expression.

She was happier than she had ever been, Casey realised as Raffa kissed her, and when he released her she realised she was still staring at him like a lovesick fool. She quickly turned her attention to the peach, to distract both of them.

'Mmm, this is delicious,' she said, juice running down her chin.

'Let me help you,' Raffa suggested. Holding her, he sucked the peach juice from her lips.

'Aren't you going to have one of your own?' She was in no hurry to let him go, and could have stared at him for ever, but there were peaches hanging from every tree. 'I must have been sleeping when you did this.'

'You ask too many questions.' Raffa stared her in the eyes. 'Why can't you just enjoy?'

'We're never going to make it into the water.'

'Who says we won't?' Raffa turned from teasing the sensitive hollow just below her chin to throwing off his robe in seconds. Standing in front of her like Hercules, he challenged, 'I'll race you.'

'You have an unfair advantage.'

He took unfair advantage of it too, diving in seconds before she arrived. He was already swimming strongly when she joined him, exclaiming in shock at the cooler water on her overheated skin. 'You said it would be warm.' She turned around, but he was nowhere to be seen.

'It is warm,' Raffa said, making her shriek as he surfaced.

'You frightened me.'

'Then may I suggest a drop of chilled juice to dilute your fear?'

'Here in the pool? You're joking—'

'No, I'm not…' Taking her by the hand, he led her through the shallows to where the waterfall tumbled into the pool, making that part of the water icy cold. 'Put your hand in here.'

Casey could see nothing beyond the wall of water, but at Raffa's insistence she thrust her hand into it.

'Now, feel around…Here, let me help you,' he shouted above the crash of spray.

The touch of Raffa's warm arm and shoulder was more than welcome, but she was determined to find it first. 'I've got it,' she exclaimed triumphantly, pulling out a large glass bottle. Champagne.

'And glasses,' Raffa prompted, taking the bottle from her.

'You must have planned this like a military campaign,' she said, bracing herself for another sortie.

'Are you complaining?' Raffa murmured dangerously close to her ear.

'Far from it,' she told him with a happy laugh.

'Then let's go and have breakfast.'

She was in over her head, Casey realised, pulling on her clothes. Losing sight of the fact that this could never last because of their relative positions in life was the least of her worries. She was deeply in love and loving every moment of this. She was committed to living the fantasy, Casey thought, following Raffa into the shallows.

And should be committed for doing this, her sensible self insisted.

Maybe, Casey thought, frowning, but in her heart she was totally committed to Raffa and to A'Qaban. How could it be otherwise, when her whole life seemed to have been leading up to this moment?

They got dressed quickly—Raffa in his robe and Casey already regretting the fact that she had scorned the robe he'd offered her in favour of fiddly trousers and a buttoned-up top. Robes were far more accommodating to still-damp bodies, Casey realised, hoiking her undergarments into some sort of order as Raffa went ahead around the sandy rim of the lagoon. He was leading her towards what might have been best described as a shady dell, if there had been oak trees instead of palms. As they rounded a rocky promontory she gasped in disbelief. 'Croissants?'

Casey stared at the feast laid out on a rug in front of them. There were even cushions to sit on, in the shade at the edge of the lagoon. On a clean linen tablecloth a mouthwatering display of fruit, bread and cheese was spread out, and everything was neatly covered in a net cloth to keep the bugs away.

'You're full of surprises,' she said, shaking her head in disbelief.

'For a wild man of the desert?' Raffa suggested dryly, throwing her a glance.

'Oh, please don't be insulted. I mean it as a compliment. But did we really bring everything here on the horse? I remember the bulging saddle bags, but I had no idea you'd brought so much.' Clapping her hands together, she stared at Raffa and then at the food.

Suddenly she saw the light. Raffa must think her really dumb, Casey concluded.

'What's wrong?' he said.

'You didn't prepare any of this, did you?' She gestured in disappointment and let her hands drop back to her sides.

'Did I say that I did?' Raffa's luminous gaze sharpened.

'You didn't have to. I presumed...' She glanced around. 'But then I'm also guilty of presuming we're alone out here. And that can't be true, can it, Raffa?'

'Does it make a difference?'

'To walking around in the nude? To swimming in the nude? To believing this is our private paradise? Yes, it does.' She moved away from him as icy dread trickled down her spine. 'You misled me,' she said, swinging around. 'I feel like I've been had. Is this how it's going to be?' She made a gesture and then stopped, the words freezing on her lips. There was no 'going to be', because there was no future for them. When was she ever going to get that into her head?

Raffa walked over to her. 'We were alone,' he said quietly. 'We were alone right up to dawn this morning, when the camel train came in with the supplies I'd asked for from the camp we visited. I wanted to do something special for you—something you would never forget.'

She'd never forget how she felt now, Casey realised. Raffa couldn't see that he didn't need to do anything for her, that he only had to be. And this was the second time she had misjudged him so badly.

Confused and full of emotion, she passed a hand across her eyes as if to wipe the debacle from her memory. 'I'm sorry.'

'Casey?'

'I'm sorry that I spoiled everything; that I always spoil everything.'

'You don't. You only feel so bad because you're mentally exhausted from wrestling with your conscience and still throbbing from our lovemaking—something life-changing for you.'

And not for him?

'Don't,' she said quietly when Raffa rested his hand on her arm. To discover she was just another notch on his bedpost would finish her. But perhaps she had needed this to bring her up short and make her face the truth. She had no alternative now but to be the one to finish this; she was in far enough. She was in love, deeply and for ever…and utterly pointlessly. Nothing Raffa could say or do would ever change that.

CHAPTER EIGHTEEN

SHE clung to business like a drowning man to a lifeline. She didn't need Raffa's encouragement to get dressed and meet the team of people who had remained so discreetly out of the way once they had proved it was possible to bring the five-star service of Raffa's hotels into the desert.

The part of her mind that wasn't mourning the loss of something that had never really existed had to be laid gently to one side as she turned her thoughts to business. She was soon fully involved in discussions with Raffa and the team, suggesting that more guides should be brought in to decide what would and would not be possible for enthusiastic amateurs to do in the desert. Like Raffa, she was determined not to make a sideshow of the desert people, but if some of them could be persuaded to become involved, at least on a part-time basis, they both felt their vision stood a good chance of becoming reality.

'Some of these men are already unofficial game wardens,' Raffa explained as they walked back to pick up their personal belongings from their temporary campsite.

'Do you think they might be prepared to extend their duties?'

'It's possible,' he said, all the time watching her thoughtfully. 'If you draw up a plan I'll make sure it's discussed.'

'I can't ask for more than that,' she said, though she couldn't hold his gaze when Raffa looked at her this time.

'We make a good team, Casey.'

As he helped her step over some rocks she willed herself to feel nothing as his strength kept her safe. It was a relief when he turned the conversation to Casey's idea for a safari camp within an hour of the city, where resident staff and a really good chef could be employed on a permanent basis.

'I like your idea,' he admitted when they reached the sheltered ledge where so much had happened.

'So does this mean I get the job?' She tried not to look at the rumpled mound of rugs on which they'd slept and made love as she spoke.

'Of course you've got the job. Do you think I would have brought you to the desert otherwise?'

Emotion welled inside her, threatening to spill out. Looking away, she bit down on her lip fiercely, as a reminder that this was all she had ever wanted. 'I don't know,' she said honestly, when her thoughts betrayed her. 'I hope I've proved I have skills as well as vision, and…' here she hesitated '…and staying power.'

'What's wrong, Casey?'

'Wrong?' The same problem she'd always had: she was a dreamer, and this had always been a business project with an interlude on the side, and now it was time to wake up. 'Nothing's wrong…I've just been worried about not making the grade, that's all—this has come as a relief.'

'Maybe you should try and contain your enthusiasm a little?' Raffa suggested dryly. 'You do still want the job, don't you?'

'Of course I do.'

As she nodded her head like an automaton Casey knew she had just come crashing back down to earth. Maybe the peaches and champagne at the oasis had something to do with it. Raffa's team arriving unannounced on site certainly had. She guessed now that Raffa had wanted to illustrate the fantasy future visitors would enjoy by proving that the impossible could be made possible. Was the intense lovemaking they had shared another example of this? In wanting to heal her, had Raffa simply chosen to prove yet again that the impossible was possible?

'Do I have to continue my search for a marketing supremo?' Raffa prompted when she remained silent, lost in thought.

'You've got one,' she said, instantly alert. 'I'll do the job for you, Raffa, and I'll do it well.' But she could give her life and soul to A'Qaban and it wouldn't bring her any closer to Raffa. She could share his bed, providing she was discreet about it, but that would never be enough for her.

'Congratulations! I'll summon the cavalry, and then we can celebrate properly.'

'The cavalry?'

'A helicopter.'

Of course. This was Raffa's life; a life she had no part in other than when it came to business.

After a few words in A'Qabani he snapped the phone shut again. 'They'll be here in ten. Yes, I know,' he said, misreading the expression on her face. 'It beats horseback, but it isn't half as much fun.'

'Okay, so I'm almost a convert,' Casey confessed, thinking that now she had made the decision to put her feelings to one side it should be easier to relax around Raffa. But it wasn't, and he was instantly concerned.

'You seem preoccupied?'

'Me? No…' She shook her head. Anything else she had to say to him could wait.

The helicopter trip to the city was smooth and uneventful. The helipad was located on the top of Raffa's office building, there he helped her out and escorted her to his suite on the top floor, where they were to discuss the finer points of her contract.

He could switch so easily from lover to employer, Casey reflected, while she was finding it hard if not impossible. He left her drinking coffee while he went to shower and change his clothes, and returned to her ten minutes later looking like an ad for Armani in a tailored business suit.

'You've done it again,' she said self-consciously.

'Done what again?' He was already going through her contract, completely unaware of how very physical and handsome he was.

'I'm a little underdressed for this,' Casey observed, glancing down at her safari suit.

'Forgive me—I should have taken you straight to your hotel, where you could have freshened up. Would you like to use the bathroom here?'

And prolong this meeting? 'No, thank you. I'll be fine,' she told him in her best business voice.

'When you sign the contract you'll have access to all that's best in A'Qaban.'

Not quite all, Casey thought as she studied the small print and tried not to look at Raffa.

By the time he had uncapped his fountain pen her mind was made up. 'There's just one thing I'd like to change.'

'Which is?' He came to look over her shoulder at the contract.

'I can do the job as well from the UK as I can from here.'

'What are you saying, Casey?' Raffa's expression darkened.

'I won't be staying.'

'I thought we'd agreed this—'

'I can market A'Qaban from anywhere in the world.' She surprised herself with the calmness of her voice. 'I can train personnel, implement change, and even source all the manpower you could possibly need from my home office.'

'A'Qaban is the home office for this job,' Raffa cut across her coldly. 'And my terms are non-negotiable. They are the most generous terms in the Gulf. I have every benefit set up for my employees that you can imagine.'

Except the only benefit she wanted—which was him. 'I'll do the job for you. Just not from here.' She couldn't live day in day out, pretending that loving Raffa, the man who was king, who could never be hers, didn't hurt.

'Non-negotiable,' Raffa rapped. 'Take it or leave it.'

She attempted to moisten her lips with a tongue turned dry. 'I'll leave it, thank you,' she said, standing up.

* * *

He was dumbfounded. He prided himself on reading people, but he had got Casey badly wrong. Her plan was good. A'Qaban needed her. And he wanted her. He had formed some vague notion, he realised now, that she would always be here, and that they would work together for the good of the country, and that in rare interludes of relaxation they would enjoy each other in every sense of the word.

'I'll take a cab.'

She was already at the door, he realized, refocusing. 'No—my driver will take you.'

'I can call a cab—really. I'd prefer to.'

His intention had always been to build Casey's confidence, and it seemed he had succeeded, even if that intention had backfired. 'As you wish…' He turned his back, trying to make sense of what was happening. He couldn't believe she was walking out on him.

She had everything packed and was ready to leave. She had checked the rooms and had only to switch the television off. It was on to keep her company. Poor company, Casey reflected, but at least there was sound and voices and life going on outside of her own small concerns to put everything in perspective. There was just one more thing she had to do. Picking up the phone, she placed her order.

He had never learned to give up, Raffa accepted, as he stood in silence by the door listening to Casey making her phone call. He didn't eavesdrop either, as a general rule, but desperate times called for desperate measures.

'Raffa—' She whirled around, a guilty expression on her face. She even hid the phone with her hand, as if she had done something terrible.

'My apologies for alarming you, but the door was open…'

'The bell boy just collected my luggage,' she explained, replacing the receiver in its nest. 'I told him I'd be right down and not to bother with the door.'

'And then you remembered a call you had to make?'

'No…not exactly.'

She still wouldn't look at him.

'It was a call I had to make before I left A'Qaban,' she said, so softly he had to strain to hear her.

She wasn't going to tell him, so he would have to repeat what he'd overheard. 'An order for pencils and colouring pads, crayons and paints for the children you met in the desert?'

The nod of her head was almost imperceptible, and then she lifted her chin to confront him. 'It's only a small thing, Raffa.'

'Small?' he frowned. 'Whose opinion are you stating now?'

'I mean on the scale of things you do here—on the scale of your proposals for spending the money we raised at the auction, for example.'

'The money *you* raised,' he corrected her.

'It's such a little thing.'

'Not for the children…'

She mulled this over before speaking, and when she raised her head to express her thoughts he thought her the loveliest and most precious creature on earth. It struck him like a knife in his heart when he saw the tears in her eyes. If he should lose her—

'I just thought we'd forgotten the small things that matter.' Mashing her lips together with embarrassment, she made a small, self-deprecating sound accompanied by an even smaller gesture. 'The little things that make life…'

'Fun?' he supplied as Casey's voice tailed away. Had he forgotten those things too?

She swallowed as their gazes held. 'There should be fun…'

She made it sound like a question and he could understand why. Beyond lust and business there hadn't been too much time for fun, and he remembered now with a wistfulness that was new to him their impulsive dance with the children in the desert.

'Yes, there *should* be fun,' he assured her. She always put others first, but who made time for Casey?

The flight Casey was supposed to be taking home to the UK had experienced an unexpected delay. Once it was clear there would be no further flights that day, and he had changed into jeans and a casual top, he persuaded Casey she might as well hitch a lift with him to the Bedouin encampment. He wanted to make sure she had the pleasure of distributing the gifts herself. He wanted her.

She was so excited. Seated next to him in the cockpit of the helicopter, he could sense her pleasure and impatience to return to the desert. It had completely obliterated her reluctance to have anything more to do with him.

He couldn't believe he had almost lost her. He couldn't believe she had been slipping through his fingers like sand while he had been obsessed by duty. It had taken Casey to prove to him that duty went far beyond the chequebook and must have a heart. She was that heart. In a few, short intense days she had broken through his emotional guard with her innocence and her goodness and integrity. She had shown him that money could never be the answer to a country's problems.

He glanced across to find her staring intently through the Plexiglass viewing panel at their feet. Children were already gathering on the ground and waving up at them.

'Be careful, Raffa.'

Her exclamation came through his headphones as he brought the helicopter down in a slow, controlled descent. 'Don't worry—the adults have seen us too.'

And the women. He'd wired ahead to warn them they were coming, and also to ask a favour.

Casey forgot all her concerns in the sheer pleasure of being back amongst the people she already felt so close to. She had never felt this much at home, she realised, watching the Bedouin teacher surrounded by her pupils. She had just handed over the art supplies, and now the teacher was deciding with the children on what should be their first project.

The children looked shyly at Casey as she left the mobile schoolroom in front of Raffa. They had stood up respectfully when he said goodbye, reminding Casey that for all his darkly glittering glamour and sex appeal Raffa was their king. And she was...

She was going home.

'That was a heavy sigh,' Raffa commented as he closed the door behind them.

'I'll miss them,' Casey admitted. 'I can't believe how much.'

'You don't have to go.'

'I think we both know I do.' She stared at him for a brief moment, wishing that life could be different sometimes—easier.

'There is no easy answer,' Raffa agreed, as if reading her mind. 'And what I'm about to suggest has never been easy for you.'

She followed his gaze down the dusty path. 'Oh, no...' She pulled a face. *Raad*, Raffa's stallion, and the smaller dapple grey she had ridden before were tethered in the shade beneath a thatched awning. 'You're kidding me.'

'You think?'

'Raffa...' Her heart turned over. She knew that look of his so well—though she had always seen it before in a very different context. She lifted her chin. 'Humour *now*?' If he was mocking her—

'Humour always.'

There were no followers, no bodyguards, no people clustered around them. They had walked away from the small group of school buildings and were hidden from sight.

'No, Raffa.' She turned her face away, but he backed her towards the nearest palm.

'Yes,' he growled, low and husky, pinning her there.

'No...'

He teased her with almost-kisses all the way down her neck,

around her ear, her cheek, and finally, somehow, her mouth. She must have turned to tell him to stop, Casey reasoned, managing to hold out for around a nano-second before she was lost. Was she supposed to resist something she wanted so badly?

'Do you forgive me?' Raffa murmured, continuing to tease her.

'Do I forgive you for making me want you so badly? No.'

'Will you stay in A'Qaban?'

'Blackmail?' she suggested when he stopped kissing her.

He gave her a look, but didn't deny it.

'Subtlety never was your strong point,' Casey observed, fighting hard not to look at Raffa's lips.

'Try this,' he said. 'You have to stay.'

'I don't *have* to do anything.'

'May I finish?'

Casey signalled her assent, but remained tensely aware of Raffa's body heat and sexual charisma; all the things she had sworn off for life, she remembered.

'A'Qaban needs you—and my people need you—here, with them—not delivering disembodied instructions from afar. Didn't you see those children's faces when you arrived?'

'Oh, that really isn't fair,' Casey protested.

'So now I've touched you?' Raffa remarked dryly.

'Only because you play dirty.'

'I play to win.'

'I don't know how I could stay.'

'You'd move in with me?' he suggested casually.

'You're short of a room-mate?' Casey said cynically.

'No, I'm short of a wife.'

CHAPTER NINETEEN

'A WIFE?' Casey looked at Raffa for a moment, and then burst out laughing. At least it had relieved the tension, she reasoned. Raffa always had had a keen sense of humour. 'Yeah, right,' she intoned dryly. 'Queen Casey. Like *that's* ever going to happen.'

'What's wrong with your name?' Raffa asked, apparently deciding to play it straight for a change. 'Though in A'Qaban you would be known by an A'Qabani name, of course. You would be free to choose something you like—something you think reflects who you are as a person…' He narrowed his eyes in thought for a moment. '*Atija*, for instance.'

'Does that mean stubborn too?' Casey said wryly, remembering the shawl Raffa had referred to as his *atija*.

'You might find out one day…if the conditions are propitious.'

'Propitious?' Casey scoffed, shaking her head. 'I can't believe you're interested in progressing this fantasy. Aren't I supposed to be the fantasist and you the realist?'

When Raffa shrugged and raised his brows in infuriating challenge, Casey knew she had to stop this before it got out of hand and she started believing it. 'You've known me—what? A week?' she reminded him.

'How long does your rule book say it takes to fall in love?'

'My rule book?' She sighed. They both knew her experience prior to A'Qaban was nil. And as for love—how could Raffa make light of love? He was discussing it as casually as he might have discussed any other statistic with her.

'I know you rather well from your personnel file,' he continued, as if all this was for real. 'And I know you even better from our close association over the past few days.'

You could say that, Casey silently conceded.

'You've been put to quite a few tests,' he reminded her.

'That's as may be—but I don't know *you*.'

'What does your heart tell you, Casey?'

Her heart? No way. Her heart had never been her best advisor.

'How did you feel when you discovered you couldn't fly home?'

Relieved. 'Anxious.' She'd go with that. Anxiety was her safest option.

She should have known Raffa would challenge her right away.

'Anxious? That doesn't sound like you, Casey. When something goes wrong you find a solution. You don't sit around feeling sorry for yourself, or…anxious.' He mocked the offending word.

'I'm anxious now because you won't let me go.' She stared pointedly at his hard-muscled arms, currently lodged either side of her face, while his fists rested against the tree trunk.

'I don't think you are,' he argued softly. 'I think you rather like it…'

'No, I don't…' She did. She adored having him look at her this way. All she wanted was for Raffa to want her as much as she wanted him.

'How did you feel when I brought you here?'

Elated. 'I was really glad the children could have their art equipment right away.'

'Now at last I believe you,' he said, pulling back. 'Was that a sigh of disappointment?' he added.

She couldn't afford to be so careless about her feelings when Raffa was around. 'It was a sigh of relief,' she informed him briskly, brushing her arms to remove the imaginary handprints he had left. The truth was he hadn't even touched her, but had held her in front of him by sheer force of will. And because she had wanted to be there, Casey admitted silently. She had been waiting…okay, hoping, for a deservedly punishing kiss—one she could really have a go at him about.

'Haven't you forgotten something?' he called after her as she started to walk away.

'Have I?' She kept on walking.

'You've got a riding lesson booked. Or…you could sit in the helicopter and wait for me to get back?'

Balling her hands into fists, she rounded on him. 'You—'

'Arrogant brute? Just a suggestion,' he said dryly. 'Why don't you let me help you mount up?'

'Because I'm quite capable of lengthening the stirrups myself.'

'So you *are* coming with me…'

A little quiver of anticipation ran through her. 'Better I know what you're doing.' Maybe. But she couldn't see what he was thinking now Raffa had started winding his *howlis* round his head. With the western jeans, boots and snug-fitting top, the black cloth over his face gave him the appearance of a brigand on the loose, and it was a struggle to ignore his particular brand of confidence as she heaved her way determinedly into the saddle.

She wouldn't have known which way they were going even with a compass and a map. The desert all looked the same to her. But Raffa didn't hesitate once. He led the way on *Raad*, keeping to the shadows beneath the dunes, and less than an hour had passed before he steered her into a place of extreme shade and surprising cool, between two towering walls of rock. The horses' hooves clattered eerily in the silence, and Casey was glad when a stream of brilliant sunlight finally illuminated an opening at the other end.

She gasped when they emerged onto an elevated plateau. They were in the foothills of the mountains somewhere, looking out over the best view she'd seen so far. The sun was at its highest point, and the splash of gold, umber and bleached white rock against the cloudless cobalt sky was quite extraordinary.

'You like it?' Raffa said, turning in the saddle.

'The colours are amazing.'

'That's one of the reasons I brought you here,' Raffa explained as Casey drew her pony to a halt alongside his stallion. 'There are no shades of grey in the desert. The colours are absolute.'

As would be any conversation they shared from this point on, Casey suspected.

They sat for a moment, enjoying the tranquillity and the beauty in front of them, with only the sound of bits being champed and bridles creaking—until, turning *Raad*'s head, Raffa encouraged the stallion down the steep rocky incline. Casey's mount followed behind, and both horses picked their way carefully, keen to make the descent. They could smell water, Casey conjectured as their ears pricked up. She could hear water running too. It was somewhere nearby, as yet unseen.

'It's an underground stream,' Raffa shouted back when she asked him about it. 'Water is more valuable than oil in the desert, and A'Qaban is rich in both those commodities.'

Another bonus for her scheme, Casey concluded. There could be nothing worse in her eyes than developing tourism at the expense of a country's natural resources.

'There's plenty of water in the desert if you know where to look,' Raffa said, hearing her gasp of surprise.

'So this is another palace?' she exclaimed, seeing the tented pavilions arranged on a sheltered sandy base in the encircling rock-walled arena.

'I thought this might give you some ideas for your tourist village,' Raffa said, turning in the saddle.

'One or two,' she admitted, as some women dressed in flowing jewel-coloured robes came out to greet them. 'What are they saying?' she asked, turning to Raffa for translation when the smiling women spoke to her in A'Qabani.

He looked at her. 'They want to make you welcome,' he said.
'Is there something wrong with that?'

'No…' Casey said, shaking her head as she started to smile.
'Nothing at all.'

Raffa went out riding while Casey gave herself up to a warm,
frothy bath, scented with something fabulous, and a massage
with oils that smelled even better. When she saw the robe the
women had brought for her to wear she had to hide a smile. Did
it follow her around, or was this sky-blue robe with its delicate
silver cross-stitch embroidery traditional Bedouin wear?

The beautiful robe could only be worn in the boudoir, Casey
concluded as the women left her. It was hardly serviceable
wear. And she was hardly your typical boudoir wench. The
fabric was the finest cloth imaginable: a cobweb, just the suggestion of a whisper against her warm, naked skin, and as such
the utmost in self-indulgence.

The women had left her with a platter of fresh fruit and a
bowl in which to rinse her hands when she had finished eating
it. And she could do all that without once moving from the soft
bank of cushions on which they had insisted she must recline.
She could get used to this.

She had a perfect view of the desert, and it wasn't long
before an image undulated in the sultry air. At first she thought
she might be imagining it, but reluctantly the shimmering heat
yielded up an indistinct form that became a man on a black
stallion…and not just any man.

She was shivering with desire even as waves of heat washed
over her. Raffa appearing like a mirage out of the vastness of
the desert was a warning to her that she could never harness the
desert's unforgiving harshness without his advice. She had to
stay in A'Qaban. There was no chance she could do her job from
the safety of an office chair in London. She watched him rein
in and spring down. Throwing the reins of the stallion to one of
the children who had come to watch his approach, he spoke to

them in A'Qabani before striding towards her. A rush of energy accompanied him as he walked into the pavilion. Unwinding his *howlis*, he tossed it onto a cushion and ruffled his hair.

'Good,' he said, giving her a scorching once-over. 'I'm going to take a swim and then I'll be right back.'

Good? She stood up, infusing limbs that had become languid with a much overdue dose of primness and purpose. 'Would you like anything to eat?' she said, stopping him mid-stride. 'Or something to drink, perhaps?'

'All of the above,' Raffa agreed, shooting her a look. 'But I want extras on the side.' He held up his hands when she started to protest. 'I'll be back in ten.'

See that you're ready? Was that what he meant? She stood transfixed as he strode away. She thought she'd been aroused before, but this was better—stronger; this was fantasy and reality clashing head on.

And it was wrong, her inner voice counselled.

How long would he be? How would she survive until he came back again? She started to pace. How much harm could one more night do? Casey reasoned as a crescent moon competed for her attention with the sun.

Raffa returned with just a towel wrapped around his waist. His body was bronzed and superbly muscled. His powerful torso, with the fearsome tattoo glistening on his still-damp skin, was something Casey knew she would never forget.

'Thank you for bringing me here, Raffa.'

'It's a shameless ploy to make you change your mind about leaving A'Qaban,' he said, swiping his wilful hair behind his ears with both hands.

'You're dripping on me.' Casey laughed as Raffa stood over her.

'I intend to do a lot more than that,' he said. Dropping down on the cushions beside her, he drew her into his arms. 'You look beautiful in A'Qabani traditional dress,' he murmured, reverently stroking the soft blue fabric.

As his knuckles grazed her peaking nipples the tiny silver cross-stitches seemed to glitter as the shadows turned from sienna to purple, as if the robe had been created for the night. There was no need for conversation, for concerns or second thoughts. Raffa simply removed his towel, tossed it away and drew her beneath him, lifting her robe above her hips in the same, fluid movement. He sank inside her, pausing only to savour the same extremes of pleasure she was experiencing.

It was enough…this was enough. It was impossible to put into words how close she felt to him. To say they were one was a cliché, but when Raffa lifted himself on his elbow so he could stare into her eyes as he began to move, she knew there would never be another night like this. Tears spilled onto her cheeks as the desert moon rose higher in the indigo sky.

'If I make you cry, I'd better stop,' Raffa warned huskily, nuzzling his sharp black stubble against her aroused neck.

'If you stop I'll howl,' she warned.

His answer was to kiss her tears away, and keep on kissing her until her rhythmic sighs filled their ears. And when holding on was impossible, he held her safe in his arms, staring deep into her eyes as she cried out his name in the throes of ecstasy.

She must have slept for a while, because she woke to find Raffa propped on one arm, looking at her. Her robe had come off some time during their lovemaking, and she was sprawled contentedly on the bank of cushions, with the light from a lantern throwing golden ribbons of light across her naked skin.

'What's this?' she murmured groggily as Raffa lifted her into his arms, kissing her brow as he wrapped a wisp of fabric around her head. 'It's my shawl!' she exclaimed, recognising it.

'An A'Qabani wedding shawl.' Raffa's darkly handsome face creased in a grin. 'Some might say it was fate that made me choose to donate it to the auction, and you to bid for it and win.'

'And some might say it isn't fair to tease me,' Casey said sensibly, drawing herself into a sitting position, keeping the lovely shawl in place around her shoulders.

'I love you, Casey Michaels,' Raffa murmured, helping her to adjust the folds of filament-fine fabric.

'You shouldn't say that.'

Raffa's brow creased. 'And why not?'

'You've already admitted this is just a ploy to keep me here in A'Qaban.'

'I don't deny it.'

'And saying I love you comes so easily to you. And please,' she said, throwing up her hands, 'don't tell me that years of experience have made it easy.'

'I'm not teasing you now. I'm serious.'

'Serious about my being funny and something of a novelty in your high-tone world?'

'That's not fair, Casey.' He cut across her. 'I think you're caring and clever, and a whole host of things that don't make me laugh.'

'I make you angry and impatient?' she suggested dryly.

'Never,' he said fiercely. 'And please don't make fun of this. I'm being serious.' Cupping her face in his hands, he asked in a fierce whisper, 'Why can't I love you for yourself?'

'Because there's not that much to love? Because your definition of love and my definition are worlds apart?'

'Why can't you believe you're worth loving, Casey?'

'Average loving between two people I can buy into; family loving I can buy into. Loving a friend—I understand that too. But you're a—'

'A king?' Raffa threw back his head and laughed.

'What's so funny?'

'I'm a man,' he said. 'A man who loves a woman. I'm a man who wants one particular woman and can think of no other woman at his side. I want you to have my babies—lots of them. And I want you to help me with the development and growth of my country. And as for love—I want you to have it all.'

'And you haven't mistaken me for someone else?'

'If you don't want to stay—'

'You'll let me go?' she said, confident he was asking her to give him the easy way out.

'No,' he argued. 'I'll make you my captive virgin of the desert.'

'It's a bit late for that.'

'But not too late to smile, to hope––and, yes, even to dream.'

'You can't see what I'm thinking behind my veil,' Casey said confidently, drawing the fabric over her face.

'Ah, but you'd be surprised at just how much your eyes can tell me.'

'The secret language of the veil,' she murmured.

'What?'

'The secret language of the veil,' Casey repeated. 'I speak it and you understand.'

'Like a true A'Qabani,' Raffa agreed, lips tugging in wry amusement as he took the veil and moved it away. 'But I prefer to look at your face, Casey Michaels. Because this is the face of the woman who's going to stand at my side as my equal, and never, ever doubt herself again.'

EPILOGUE

THEY chose a Bedouin ceremony. Or had the Bedouin chosen it for them? Casey wondered, stealing a glance through the heavy curtain over her bridal tent. It hardly mattered; she felt happy here—as if she belonged.

The women whose task it was to dress her were already gathering in small excited groups, adding to her own almost unbearable sense of anticipation. Her parents had been over in the country for a week and loved everything about the desert kingdom. They were already planning to seek instruction at the hands of the women who understood the seductive techniques of the silken veil.

The famed Bedouin hospitality and cultural heritage, together with the A'Qabani traditions of music, dance and art, had quickly won over all Casey's friends and family, and if her parents found the thought of their daughter becoming a queen bewildering, they hid it well.

But who could resist Raffa? Casey wondered, watching him lead some of his men off to the desert on horseback at a gallop. He had been doing this for the past week—no doubt to work off some of his surplus energy. As tradition demanded he had been forced to keep away from her during this time. And if he was finding it hard, she was going mad for him, Casey thought dry-mouthed, pulling back from her vantage point.

Fortunately the women arrived at that moment to distract her.

They were going to decorate her hands and feet with intricate swirls of henna, and she had made hot sweet mint tea and *gahwa*, the intensely aromatic A'Qabani coffee, to welcome them. This *Laylat al Henna* ceremony was their gift to her of beauty, luck and health, and while they gathered in the privacy of her pavilion, like so many vivid butterflies, Casey found herself hoping some of their natural grace would rub off. She needed all the henna she could get, Casey concluded as the women got to work.

Musicians outside the tent provided a rhythmic background for these activities, playing an upbeat riff on the *dalouka*, a big drum, and on the one-stringed *rababa* violin. Some of the men must be dancing too, Casey realised, hearing their guttural shouts and the crack of whips as they stamped their feet on the hard, hot earth. There had been a riot of music and colourful dancing pretty much non-stop in the Bedouin encampment since Raffa had finally persuaded her that he was actually proposing she do more than stay in the country to work. There were banners and pennants everywhere, and even the horses boasted jostling tassels and silver bells on their saddle cloths, along with yet more silver in the form of coins on their gleaming leather bridles and brow bands.

And the bride? She had been bathed in scented water and massaged with sweet-smelling unguents during the traditional *Al Aadaa*, while the women teased Raffa until he agreed to pay, as tradition demanded, for their decorating his bride. And now this…

Casey examined her henna-decorated hands and feet in awe. 'I have never seen anything more beautiful. You're amazing,' she exclaimed.

'Don't commit yourself to that statement until you have seen this,' one of the young women told her.

'What is it?'

'The gifts that have arrived from your husband…'

Casey opened the stunning golden casket cautiously. Her eyes widened as she drew a sharp intake of breath. The fabulous sapphire necklace she had seen in Raffa's strong room was there, together with bracelets and earrings, and even ankle chains of blue-white diamond links. But beneath it all there was a simple roll of quite modern looking paper. Tied with raffia, there was a message tucked into its bow. Pulling it out, she read, 'I wanted to give you the jewellery, but I know you'll like this best. R.'

Still frowning, Casey glanced up to see the expectant faces of the women gathered around her. 'I've no idea what this can be,' she confided as she carefully brought out the scroll.

'Why don't you open it and find out?' one of them prompted as they all exchanged excited glances.

'You know, don't you?' Casey challenged them, starting to laugh. The young woman who had spoken out was the school-teacher. She unrolled the sheet of paper carefully to find the children had drawn and painted a picture of Raffa and herself, hand in hand. 'When did they do this?'

'The same day you visited them,' the teacher told her, hiding her smiles behind her hand. 'It was the one picture they could all agree on.'

'They knew? They knew before I did?' Casey scratched her head in a most un-queenly manner.

'Children know far more than we give them credit for,' the young woman told her, already reaching for the fabulous jewels Raffa had sent as a wedding gift. 'As you will find out…'

She was dressed in a robe of crimson silk, with silver coins decorating the chiffon veil covering her hair. More silver twinkled at her ankles and on her wrist, and round her neck the rich blue sapphires competed with the azure of her eyes. She was taken to Raffa's black camelhair tent on a freshly sham-pooed and muzzled camel, sitting on a *houdach*, a specially adapted and ultra-comfortable saddle. She found Raffa waiting for her at the entrance. Dressed in a simple black robe, his head uncovered and his earring glinting in the late-afternoon sun, he might have been any A'Qabani waiting for his bride—apart from the very wicked expression in his eyes. That was how he liked it and how she liked it too—no pomp and ceremony, just Raffa, the man, and the woman he loved. Theirs was a marriage of equals, Raffa had told her, his slumberous eyes turning solemn for once.

He helped her dismount, carefully arranging the folds of her robe and her veil, while the crowd stood hushed and tense around them. The touch of his hand was electrifying. She'd missed him. She'd missed his strength, his humour, his fast mind and his sex. However shallow that made her, she'd missed that most of all, Casey realised wryly as Raffa led her by the hand towards the elders of the village who were to perform the age old rites.

'Sheikha.'

'Sheikha Casey?' Casey whispered with concern to Raffa, as the old man began to intone the words of the marriage ceremony. Had Raffa forgotten something? She began to worry when he didn't respond. What she hadn't realised was that he would address the crowd before the ceremony was over…

Casey had heard love expressed in words before, and she was addicted to love poetry, but to hear Raffa speak of her as his gift, his *atija*, a gift that had come to him unexpectedly and that he wanted to share with his people, was more than she had ever expected to hear from him.

'Sheikha *Atija*,' he said, taking Casey's right hand in his when his oration had ended. 'If you don't like the name,' he whispered close to her ear, 'you can choose another one.'

'I love it,' she assured him—full of delighted surprise. 'Like the shawl you donated to the auction, it's what I am—sensible and serviceable.'

'Keep that last thought in mind,' Raffa murmured without a flicker of expression on his face to betray the path his thoughts were taking. 'I'm well overdue a service…'

'So, are you happy with your new name?' Raffa asked Casey later, when they were lazing on their enormous marriage bed in a secluded pavilion.

'I'm very pleased with it.'

'That's good.' Winding a lock of her glossy blonde hair around his finger to bring her close, he explained, 'As that is the case, honour demands you please me in return.'

'Oh, well, I'm sure I'll think of something.'

'I'm sure you will. Would you like to put my honour to the test?'

'I intend to do so constantly,' she assured him.

* * * * *

Turn the page for an exclusive extract from

THE PLAYBOY SHEIKH'S VIRGIN STABLE-GIRL
by
Sharon Kendrick

Claimed by the sheikh—for her innocence!

Polo-playing Sheikh Prince Kaliq Al'Farisi loves his women as much as his horses. They're wild, willing and he's their master!

Stable girl Eleni is a local Calistan girl. Raised by her brutal father on the horse racing circuit, she feels unlovable. When her precious horses are given to Sheikh Kaliq she *refuses* to be parted from them.

The playboy sheikh is determined to bed her, and when he realizes she's a virgin the challenge only becomes more interesting. However, Kaliq is torn; his body wants Eleni, yet his heart wants to protect her....

"WHAT WOULD YOU SAY, MY DAUGHTER, if I told you that a royal prince was coming to the home of your father?"

She would say that he *had* been drinking, after all. But never to his face, of course. If Papa was having one of his frequent flights of fancy then it was always best to play along with it.

Eleni kept her face poker-straight. "A royal prince, Papa?" she questioned gravely.

"Yes, indeed!" He pushed his face forward. "The Prince Kaliq Al'Farisi," he crowed, "is coming to my house to play cards with me!"

Her father had gone insane! These were ideas of grandeur run riot! And what was Eleni to do? What if he continued to make such idle boasts in front of the men who were sitting waiting to begin the long night of card-playing? Surely that would make him a laughingstock and ruin what little reputation he had left.

"Papa," she whispered urgently, "I beg you to think clearly. What place would a royal prince have *here?*"

But she was destined never to hear a reply, even though his mouth had opened like a puppet's, for there came the sound of distant hooves. The steady, powerful thud of horses as they thundered over the parched sands. On the still, thick air the muffled beat grew closer and louder until it filled Eleni's ears like the sound of the desert wolves that howled at the silver moon when it was at its fullest.

Toward them galloped a clutch of four horses, and as Eleni watched, one of them broke free and surged forward like a black stream of oil gushing out of the arid sand. For a moment, she stood there, transfixed—for this was as beautiful and as reckless a piece of riding as she had ever witnessed.

Illuminated by the orange-gold of the dying sun, she saw a colossus of a man with an ebony stallion between his thighs that he urged on with a joyful shout. The man's bare head was as dark as the horse he rode and his skin gleamed like some bright and burnished metal. Robes of pure silk clung to the hard sinews of his body. As he approached, Eleni could see a face so forbidding that some deep-rooted fear made her wonder if he had the power to turn to dust all those who stood before him.

And a face so inherently beautiful that it was as if all the desert flowers had bloomed at once.

It was then that Eleni understood the full and daunting truth. Her father's bragging *had* been true, and riding toward their humble abode was indeed Prince Kaliq Al'Farisi. Kaliq the daredevil, the lover of women, the playboy, the gambler and irresponsible twin son of Prince Ashraf. The man it was said could make women moan with pleasure simply by looking at them.

She had not seen him since she was a young girl in the crowds watching the royal family pass by. Back then, he had been doing his military service and wearing the uniform of the Calistan Navy. And back then he had been an arresting young man, barely out of his twenties. But now—a decade and a half on—he was at the most magnificent peak of his manhood, with a raw and beautiful masculinity that seemed to shimmer from his muscular frame.

"By the wolves that howl!" Eleni whimpered, and ran inside the house.

* * * * *

HARLEQUIN *Presents*

TWO CROWNS, TWO ISLANDS, ONE LEGACY

*A royal family torn apart by pride and lust for power,
reunited by purity and passion*

THE ROYAL HOUSE *of* KAREDES

Pick up the next adventure in this passionate series!

THE PLAYBOY SHEIKH'S VIRGIN STABLE-GIRL
by Sharon Kendrick, August 2009

THE PRINCE'S CAPTIVE WIFE
by Marion Lennox, September 2009

THE SHEIKH'S FORBIDDEN VIRGIN
by Kate Hewitt, October 2009

THE GREEK BILLIONAIRE'S INNOCENT PRINCESS
by Chantelle Shaw, November 2009

THE FUTURE KING'S LOVE-CHILD
by Melanie Milburne, December 2009

RUTHLESS BOSS, ROYAL MISTRESS
by Natalie Anderson, January 2010

THE DESERT KING'S HOUSEKEEPER BRIDE
by Carol Marinelli, February 2010

Eight volumes to collect and treasure!

International Billionaires

*Life is a game of power and pleasure.
And these men play to win!*

BLACKMAILED INTO THE GREEK TYCOON'S BED
by **Carol Marinelli**

When ruthless billionaire Xante Rossi catches
mousy Karin red-handed, he designs a way to save
her from scandal. But she'll have to earn
the favor—in his bedroom!

Book #2846

Available August 2009

Look for the last installment of
International Billionaires from Harlequin Presents!

THE VIRGIN SECRETARY'S IMPOSSIBLE BOSS
by *Carole Mortimer*
September 2009

www.eHarlequin.com

HP12846

NIGHTS *of* PASSION

One night is never enough!

*These guys know what they want
and how they're going to get it!*

NAUGHTY NIGHTS IN THE MILLIONAIRE'S MANSION
by Robyn Grady

Millionaire businessman Mitch Stuart wants no
distractions…until he meets Vanessa Craig.
Mitch will help her financially, but bewitching
Vanessa threatens his corporate rule: do not mix
business with pleasure….

Book #2850

Available August 2009

Look for more of these hot stories throughout the
year from Harlequin Presents!

ROYAL AND RUTHLESS

Royally bedded, regally wedded!

A Mediterranean majesty, a Greek prince, a desert king and a fierce nobleman—with any of these men around, a royal bedding is imminent!

And when they're done in the bedroom, the next thing to arrange is a very regal wedding!

Look for all of these fabulous stories available in August 2009!

Innocent Mistress, Royal Wife #65
by ROBYN DONALD

The Ruthless Greek's Virgin Princess #66
by TRISH MOREY

The Desert King's Bejewelled Bride #67
by SABRINA PHILIPS

Veretti's Dark Vengeance #68
by LUCY GORDON

REQUEST YOUR FREE BOOKS!

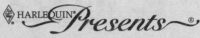 HARLEQUIN *Presents*

PASSION GUARANTEED SEDUCTION

2 FREE NOVELS PLUS 2 FREE GIFTS!

YES! Please send me 2 FREE Harlequin Presents® novels and my 2 FREE gifts (gifts are worth about $10). After receiving them, if I don't wish to receive any more books, I can return the shipping statement marked "cancel". If I don't cancel, I will receive 6 brand-new novels every month and be billed just $4.05 per book in the U.S. or $4.74 per book in Canada. That's a savings of close to 15% off the cover price! It's quite a bargain! Shipping and handling is just 50¢ per book*. I understand that accepting the 2 free books and gifts places me under no obligation to buy anything. I can always return a shipment and cancel at any time. Even if I never buy another book, the two free books and gifts are mine to keep forever.   106 HDN EYRQ 306 HDN EYR2

Name	(PLEASE PRINT)	
Address		Apt. #
City	State/Prov.	Zip/Postal Code

Signature (if under 18, a parent or guardian must sign)

Mail to the Harlequin Reader Service:
IN U.S.A.: P.O. Box 1867, Buffalo, NY 14240-1867
IN CANADA: P.O. Box 609, Fort Erie, Ontario L2A 5X3

Not valid to current subscribers of Harlequin Presents books.

Are you a current subscriber of Harlequin Presents books and want to receive the larger-print edition? Call 1-800-873-8635 today!

* Terms and prices subject to change without notice. Prices do not include applicable taxes. Sales tax applicable in N.Y. Canadian residents will be charged applicable provincial taxes and GST. Offer not valid in Quebec. This offer is limited to one order per household. All orders subject to approval. Credit or debit balances in a customer's account(s) may be offset by any other outstanding balance owed by or to the customer. Please allow 4 to 6 weeks for delivery. Offer available while quantities last.

Your Privacy: Harlequin Books is committed to protecting your privacy. Our Privacy Policy is available online at www.eHarlequin.com or upon request from the Reader Service. From time to time we make our lists of customers available to reputable third parties who may have a product or service of interest to you. If you would prefer we not share your name and address, please check here. ☐

HP09R

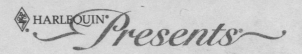

Coming Next Month

Plus, look out for the fabulous new collection
Royal and Ruthless from Harlequin® Presents® EXTRA: